We're Getting

~~Married~~ Murdered

By Carole Lynn Jones

We're Getting ~~Married~~ Murdered

This one is for the believers

*"When someone believes in you,
you start believing in yourself."
Credit Sarah Paulson*

Other Melody Shore Mysteries
by Carole Lynn Jones

This New Job's Murder (collection of five novella-length mysteries. Published by Flying Ketchup Press, 2022)

All I Want for Christmas is for You to Leave Town (short fiction available on Amazon, 2022)

Children's Books

*The High-Flying, Water-Skiing, Magician Named Worm
The Hard-Working, Dirt-Moving, Garden-Helper
Named Worm*

WE'RE GETTING ~~MARRIED~~ MURDERED

I was standing in the lobby of my employer, The Peaceful Rest Funeral Home, my eyes adjusting to the lamp-lit room, when the entryway door behind me burst open.

"I need help."

A tall, curvy-hipped, blond-haired woman wearing cat eyeglasses and a floppy sun hat stumbled in and across the funeral home lobby. She tripped, fell into a large ceramic planter holding a Peace Lily, righted herself, and collapsed into one of our high wing-back chairs. Her arms hung limp at her sides, and the eco-friendly bag she was carrying toppled to the ground. A head of lettuce and two limes rolled out.

"Stephanie? Wow, it's so great to see you...Wait. Are you okay? You don't look good."

I rushed to my old friend's side and touched the exposed skin below her silk-covered arm. She felt clammy.

"Someone...kill...me...Melody," Stephanie said, her voice barely above a whisper.

She slid from the chair to the carpeted floor, her body shaking in spasms.

"What? Who? Oh my gosh. This is for real. You're not faking." My retro-red sunglasses dropped from my hand. "Mr. Snugg, Alex, J.J., anybody! Call 911."

The funeral home fell silent.

They're at that Mortuary Science convention. Oh my gosh! It's just me!

I pulled my cell from my purse. My finger punched in the three numbers.

"911. What's your emergency?"

"I need the paramedics right away! This is Melody Shore calling from The Peaceful Rest Funeral Home on Republic Street in Pleasantview."

"What is the problem, miss?"

"A woman, a former friend, a classmate. She…I don't know what's wrong. I just returned from lunch when she came through the door and collapsed to the ground."

I looked down at Stephanie.

"Stephanie, are you okay? Please be okay."

She was whiter than the mortcloth draping the caskets at the funeral home. I checked for breathing or a pulse. *None.*

"Send help now! I'm going to start CPR."

I laid down the phone and began the technique I had learned in a certification class the previous spring.

Six long minutes later, the paramedics arrived and took over. My efforts to resuscitate Stephanie were futile. Her body went into a series of convulsions, and right in front of my glass fishbowl office, on Arthur Snugg's new, plush, red carpet, she passed away.

Russell handed me a cup of coffee. My hand shook, the warm liquid sloshing over the rim.

"Mel, maybe you should set that down and take a few deep breaths," Russell said.

Russell is my boyfriend. We started dating last year when I moved back home to Pleasantview. He is the sergeant for our local police department and has waves of curly dark hair and Irish whiskey brown eyes that I love to stare into. We got to know each other when the husband of one of our deceased decided he should test out our freezer cooler by putting my body in it. Russell quickly discovered that the funeral business isn't as dull as he imagined.

"No. The coffee is warming me up." My hands tightly gripped the mug, and I took a small sip as I paced the room. "Oh, Russell! This is horrible. I haven't seen Stephanie in eight years, and now she died right at my feet."

Russell placed my green swing jacket over my shoulders.

"Tell me about Stephanie Gregor."

We both turned toward the lobby and silently watched the coroner wheel her sheet-clad body out on his gurney.

"We went to school together. We attended all twelve years of school together." I sniffed loudly.

"You went to school together for twelve years," Russell repeated, removing his field notebook from his jacket pocket.

"Yeah, in high school, she was in my circle of friends." I inhaled deeply, blew out a breath, and repeated my calming breathing technique. "Although I could never figure out why. As we grew up, she was drop-dead gorgeous." I grimaced at my choice of words.

Russell wiped a tear that was escaping down my cheek.

"You're beautiful," he whispered. "Go on. When was the last time you saw her?"

"Well, let me think. Stephanie and I, actually most of my high school friends, went away to college and then came home that first year or two and met up a few times, but our visits became less frequent, and when I came home after that, it was mostly just to see my mom. What is she doing here? Our ten-year reunion was last year."

"I don't remember you telling me about it. Did you go?"

"No. Claire went and said that not many attended. It was a picnic down at Pleasantview Park, and only about 20 people from our class of 122 made it. I was living in Pittsburgh and couldn't come home." I sat down at my desk and gazed out into the empty funeral home lobby. "But that was before my dream job and life collapsed."

"I'm one glad guy that you moved back," Russell said, lightly rubbing my shoulders. When I turned to face him, he gave me a quick wink.

"You've made a great life here again, Mel. And besides me, your mom, and Mr. Snugg, I know Claire is over the moon that you are back in town."

"My mother. I'm not going to tell her until we find out what happened to Stephanie. Once my mom hears, no one needs to watch the news."

"She means well," Russell said.

"The woman should have been a broadcaster. She doesn't even need a microphone. I need to call Claire, though." I checked my butterfly leather strap watch. It read 2:00. My shoulders drooped.

"You're not going to call her either?" Russell asked.

"No, she had a meeting with a new buyer in the afternoon." I took another sip of coffee.

Claire was my best friend in high school, and when I returned home, we reconnected and have been inseparable ever since. She owns Claire's Cottage, a resale shop brimming with vintage clothing and accessories on Fifth Street in the heart of Pleasantview.

"I don't want to break the news to Claire and ruin her day. I'll wait until tomorrow."

"Yeah, there is nothing either one of you can do for Stephanie now," Russell said.

"Look at this. Stephanie had an appointment here today." I handed Russell my "Cats in Hats" calendar. "I saw Mr. Snugg's note while you were talking to the paramedics."

"This is your appointment calendar?" Russell's brow wrinkled up as he squinted at my desktop calendar, a four-by-five block of paper with three-quarters of it taken up by a picture of a Himalayan cat with a pillbox hat perched on its head. "You don't have your appointments and schedule on a computer?"

"Yes, we do, but Mr. Snugg has yet to figure out how to post to it, and Alex and J.J. haven't even tried. I set one up for all of us a month ago." I pointed at Snugg's untidy, barely legible writing. "It says 1:30 appointment, Stephanie Gregor. Snugg and the twins are at a mortuary science convention this weekend. He must have forgotten to tell me I was to handle his appointment."

"Another thing to add to your 'Why Snugg Needs Me and Doesn't Pay Me Enough' list," Russell said, returning to rubbing my shoulders.

I picked up the list that Russell was referring to from my desk, wrote "handles appointments without explanation," and put it away in my drawer. I had hoped to have a much-needed discussion with Arthur Snugg about my job when he returned.

"Russell, she is too young to be making funeral home appointments." I folded my hands in my lap, attempting to curb my shaking.

"Maybe someone in her family passed away," Kenneth, Russell's second-in-command, said.

"Yeah, maybe. But she's an only child. Her mom is deceased, and her dad lives out of town. Even if he passed, I doubt she would bring him back to bury them together. Her parents had a nasty divorce. We are the only funeral home in town, though."

I walked to the lobby, picked up her tote bag and strewn about groceries, and handed them to Kenneth. A square white envelope fell from the bag.

A glove-clad Kenneth picked up the envelope and handed it to Russell, who turned it over and checked the seal. Finding it sealed, he reached for my mother-of-pearl letter opener and sliced it open.

"This is a sad game of hot potato," I said with a sigh.

"Maybe this will explain why she had an appointment. Give us an idea of why she is back in town." Russell held the envelope up like a game show host.

The envelope interior was lined in navy-blue foil.

"Almost matches Pleasantview's school colors."

My thoughts of Stephanie growing up, high school, and my attempt at saving her played in my mind as Russell pulled a single sheet of cardstock from the envelope. He stared at it for a moment, cleared his throat, and began to read out loud.

"We're Getting Married"

Saturday, June 8th – 7:00 p.m. – Admiral Hotel.

> *Brandon Hoff and Rachel Grey request the honor of your presence as they tie the knot. We are sailing into matrimony, and we want you to join in the fun. We hope you can attend.*

I took the invite from his hand. At the bottom of the invitation were two interlocking anchors, and Brandon and Rachel's names were written below in calligraphy.

Russell looked quizzically at me, and I burst into tears. He handed me a tissue.

"You know Brandon and Rachel?" he asked.

"Yes, more friends from school. My mom and Rachel's mom used to be in a book club together until Mrs. Grey said my mom had to read at least one book a year to attend. She's the club president, and my mom mostly went to gossip and drink wine."

"Sounds like your mom."

"Rachel and I lost touch, too. Oh, Russell, I'm a horrible friend."

"No, you're not, Mel. Life changes. I'm sorry about your friend, but I still need to ask you some questions. Can you tell me your conversation with Stephanie and what happened before she collapsed?" His voice turned from consoling to serious as he readied his pen.

"She came into the funeral home and fell to the ground. We didn't have any conversation. I did CPR until the paramedics arrived." Tears cascaded down my cheeks. Russell put down his pen, closed his notebook, and handed me the box of tissues.

"This is awful. I have to call Mr. Snugg."

I wiped my face, took a few deep breaths, and dialed my boss. He answered on the fourth ring.

"Mr. Snugg, I'm sorry to bother you."

"No bother, Melody. We're having a late lunch. The body wasn't ready."

"What I am about to say will kill your appetite," I whispered.

"Huh?"

"Mr. Snugg, I've got bad news," I said, my voice breaking.

"What happened?" Snugg asked.

"Someone died here this morning." I sniffed and wiped my runny nose.

"Melody, you sound like you are getting laryngitis. What are you trying to say? Do you need the removers to go pick someone up? You have the authority to phone them. They will stow the body in the receiving room, and I will handle things when I return."

"No, Mr. Snugg, you aren't understanding. I'm not sick. Someone died here."

"Melody, we have dead people every day. It's my business."

"Mr. Snugg, this woman was alive when she walked through the door. An old friend of mine. She came in the door and passed away at my feet." I looked down miserably at my tan, leather Mary Janes.

"That is troublesome, Melody. Are you okay?"

"Yes. The police are here."

"Russell?"

"Yes, Mr. Snugg. Russell is here. I'm sure he wants to talk to you." I glanced toward Russell. He nodded. "But I wanted to talk to you first."

"Was there an accident? She didn't fall, did she? I repaired that broken front step right after winter. Wait, did she fall into that hole I told the twins a month ago to take care of? The 12' x 8' one they dug by mistake for John Firestone, who was cremated, and the family wanted the ashes."

"No, Mr. Snugg. It wasn't a physical accident here at the funeral home or the cemetery. She walked in the door, fell into one of the lobby chairs, and collapsed to the floor. I did CPR until the paramedics arrived, but she was gone."

"This is very upsetting," Snugg muttered.

"Mr. Snugg, the woman was Stephanie Gregor. The 1:30 appointment. Why did she have an appointment?" I held my breath.

"I don't know, Melody. She asked for an appointment with you."

"Oh my gosh!" I gasped.

Snugg didn't make the appointment and then passed it to me. Stephanie made the appointment to see me. She is in town for the wedding and delivering my invite? A week before the wedding? Why didn't Rachel and Brandon mail it? I'm sure if they didn't know my address, my mother would have gladly given it to them.

"Melody, don't get yourself upset," Snugg said.

"Hey, Mel," J.J., Arthur Snugg's nephew hollered into the phone, "Alex and I scored tickets to this weekend's convention."

"You two didn't score anything," Snugg said sternly. "I covered the cost of your attendance. These classes are mandatory for the mortuary science program you are pursuing. Now, if you would please, I need to talk to Melody."

"Young blood to represent Old Peaceful," Alex, J.J.'s twin brother, shouted in the background.

"Speaking of representing, did you bring your trunks, Uncle A?" J.J. bellowed.

"Cannonball time!" the twins yelled in unison.

"I will deflate more than those flamingo rafts you two call personal flotation devices if you both aren't in class," Snugg said firmly. "And you need to be dressed properly. You cannot wear khaki shorts and polo shirts with palm trees and pineapple skull faces on them. Go get ready. Our session on applying makeup is at 4:00 p.m. today." Arthur Snugg sighed. "Melody, please put Russell on. I will talk to you when we return."

I sat quietly while Russell spoke to Snugg. He questioned him and jotted down notes about how Stephanie had phoned last week and asked to make an appointment. When he asked Snugg whether he knew the deceased, Stephanie Gregor, I stood and began to pace my tiny office.

"Yes, Melody is shaken. Yes, I agree. She should go home. I'll tell her to forward the phone to you. Yes, that's all the questions I have for now. We will be in touch once the autopsy is complete. Thank you for your time, Arthur," Russell said.

I motioned for Russell to hand the phone back to me.

"Mr. Snugg, I hope this doesn't interfere with your conference. I know how important it is to you."

Silence. Arthur Snugg had already hung up.

"I've done all I can do for today," Russell said, picking up his notebook and looking around the empty funeral home. "Let's get you away from this place and into your apartment. I'll drive Blue Betty."

Blue Betty is my Jeep. Like Russell, she has been there for me at my best and my worst.

Outside my office window, I could see Kenneth in the remaining police car pulling out onto Republic Street. Russell picked up my kiss-lock satchel bag and held out his hand for me. I forwarded the phone to Snugg's, then together we walked to the door and I flipped the sign to closed.

When we arrived at my garage-loft apartment on Pine Street, Russell ordered tacos from Tina's Taco Bar down the street. Then, he went straight to the kitchen cupboard and set up a makeshift bar on my counter. After both of us silently downed Captain and Cokes, he slipped into the bathroom and filled my tub with water and bath salts.

Leading me into the bathroom, Russell wrapped his arms around me and hugged me tightly.

"I'll be sleeping here tonight in case you need me," he said.

When I exited the bath, I was still reeling from the day's events, but at least I was home, and my body felt relaxed, even if my mind wouldn't shut off. Russell was in the kitchen, a Mexican dinner lay on my table. The smell of cilantro, tortillas, and queso did nothing for me, however. I ate two tacos, and after two mindless hours of magazine reading and TV channel changing, he tucked me into bed.

When I awoke on Saturday morning, Russell was gone, but he left a note.

"Had to leave early. Made coffee. Saved you a donut. Fed cat. Call me."

He signed it with a heart.

My cat, Shady, meowed loudly and paced in front of his empty food bowl.

"Sorry, Shady. Russell tipped me off." I rubbed under my tuxedo cat's chin. He gave a low, soft meow and jumped up to his window perch, refusing to acknowledge me, choosing bird-watching over cat-cuddling.

I picked up the phone and called Russell. It went to voicemail.

"I'm feeling a little better. Thanks for the jelly donut," I said when prompted to speak after the beep. "I'm going to head into work and catch up on some things…since yesterday was a total nightmare."

When I got to The Peaceful Rest, I couldn't work. I sat staring at the floor where I had attempted CPR for the long six minutes it took Pleasantview's first responders to arrive.

I was about to call Arthur Snugg when Claire burst through the door and enveloped me in one of her feel-good bear hugs. She was dressed in a breezy, floor-length, daisy-print dress, and the cool cotton felt soft on my arms. I inhaled a whiff of Claire's signature 'Beachy' perfume. The smell of coconut and jasmine filled my nostrils.

"I was driving by when I saw Blue Betty parked in the lot. Let me guess, Snugg has you buried in work again." Claire giggled at her humor, and then she peered around. "Come with me to the store. I got some new dresses that are killer." She pulled from her vintage gypsy beaded bag an envelope and waved it around.

"Claire, you aren't going to believe who died here on me."

"Wait. What? Slow down, Melody. Here?" Claire sat down in my spare office chair; the envelope centered on her lap. "I thought everyone was dead at Old Peaceful."

"Very funny, Claire. No, Stephanie Gregor died," I said softly.

"Stephanie Gregor? You're kidding, right? Someone else with the same name as the Stephanie Gregor from high school?" Claire looked at me, her eyes wide, searching mine. Her hand robotically put the envelope back into her bag.

"Yeah, I can't believe it, Claire."

I explained how Stephanie burst through the door and collapsed, and how I gave her CPR until the paramedics arrived.

"Oh, Melody. That is so sad. Our old friend. I stopped here to talk about Brandon and Rachel's wedding. Does anyone else from the group know?" Claire pulled the envelope back out of her bag and removed an invitation matching the one found on Stephanie.

"I don't know. Claire, when did you get that?"

She handed it to me. I studied the envelope and realized it was postmarked and had Claire's name and address written in calligraphy across the front.

"I didn't get one in my mail. Stephanie had one in her bag. Maybe for me?" I handed Claire back her invitation.

"She had your invite? That's odd. Mine came in the mail about two weeks ago." Claire fingered the corners of the envelope and read out loud the postmark date.

"Claire, you really need to open your mail quicker."

"Why? This is the first non-bill or solicitation I've gotten in months." Claire fanned herself with the invitation.

"I should get in touch with Rachel and Brandon. But I don't feel it's right until I know more. Do you know did they still keep in touch with Stephanie?" I reached over and stopped Claire's waving hand.

"They must have if she had your invite." Claire carefully laid the invite on my desk.

"You're right. I'm not thinking clearly. Yesterday was too overwhelming. I need to talk to Russell. I hope by now the autopsy report is back, and I hate to say it, but let's hope she had some preexisting condition. I don't want to think that someone did something to her." I could feel my jaw clenching as I bit down hard on my closed lips.

"What? Don't be silly, Melody. Who would hurt Stephanie?"

"Well, in high school, she sure did know how to make people upset." I exhaled a large breath.

"Yeah, sure she flirted and stole a boyfriend or two away, but that was ten years ago. You are uber-stressed from witnessing her pass away. It's so sad and shocking, but I'm sure it was a health condition. Or maybe an aneurysm. Those can kill you instantly."

"She caused more than a few problems in relationships, that's for sure. But you're right. I'm overthinking. Let's wait until we hear from Russell." I walked to the coat rack outside my office and put on my sweater. "All of a sudden, I have a chill."

"How did Stephanie look? Wait, don't answer. That's morbid. I mean, before she died. Did she look as good as in high school?" Claire asked.

"Before she died? I don't know. Her hair is still long. Remember that poem Jake wrote for her in creative writing class? 'Stephanie has eyes the color of Pleasantview Lake and teeth white like the clouds.'" I sighed loudly and collapsed back into my office chair.

"Melody, I wish I had your curly hair."

Claire is taller than I am with long, straight, brown hair, high cheekbones that won't quit, and piercing blue eyes.

"Yeah, but not the glasses and braces I wore throughout most of high school."

"Don't be so insecure. Most of us were awkward then. Look at us now."

I straightened my back and looked down at my teal and pink tulip swing dress and black Mary Janes.

"I wonder if she and Jake are…or I guess now that she's gone…were still together?" I picked up a binder clip and snapped together assorted casket brochures.

"Jake Evans. You always crushed on him and his wavy blond sailor hair. Remember when he asked you to float around in a Sunfish out on Pleasantview Lake."

"I should have gone with him on that boat even if I'm not the best swimmer."

"Yeah, when Julie and him broke up, you should have made a play for him. Did you know she's a chiropractor now over in Duncan?"

"Wonder if she goes by Dr. Paine?" I twisted from side to side stretching my back.

"She does. But, if it were me, I think I would change my last name," Claire said.

"I hope Russell finds out what happened soon so I can try and get a hold of everyone before the wedding." I picked up my phone and checked it. "No word yet."

"Yeah, if I had known yesterday, I could have told Jules."

"Jules?" My eyebrows wrinkled in confusion.

"Julie Paine. You know, we were just talking about her."

"You talked to Julie yesterday?" My phone slipped from my hand to the floor. Claire picked it up and handed it back.

"She was my new buyer. Remember I told you. She treated me to drinks after she bought the cutest black cocktail dress and gloves at my shop for the wedding. She purchased two other complete outfits, too."

"I knew you had a new buyer, but I didn't know it was Julie."

"She said she wanted to surprise everyone. Surprised me for sure." Claire gave me a tight-lipped smile.

"You two went for drinks and didn't call me?" My voice rose an octave.

"You usually spend Friday nights with Russell. Mondays are our nights together. You're my margarita Monday partner."

"Claire, I love our MMs, but I would have gone."

"I'm sorry, Melody. It wasn't planned. She invited me at the store."

"How is Julie?" I tore yesterday's page, May 31, from my calendar. Snugg's handwriting noting Stephanie's appointment glaring back at me as my trembling hand tossed the page in the garbage.

"She's great. I better text her and tell her what's happened." Claire pulled her phone from her purse and began to push buttons. "Now, where's that favorite button?"

"You have her number in your phone favorites?" I looked at my best friend with wide eyes.

On the same day I am trying to save an old friend, but can't, another is stepping back into Claire's life and her phone's favorites directory.

I turned around and busied myself with the items in my file cabinet so Claire wouldn't see the tears forming in my eyes. "Claire, what did you two talk about? Did she mention Stephanie or anyone else from school?"

"Not Stephanie directly, no. But you know, old times, the upcoming wedding. I didn't even know I was invited until Jules told me to check my mail. We were dancing and laughing about some of our old dances." Claire stood and began to shake her hips and dance. Then she stopped mid-dance step.

"This doesn't feel right. It's so sad about Stephanie. Remember the whole drama when Julie didn't pursue Tim McCoy because she thought Stephanie liked him? Stephanie and Julie were so close. I bet Jules is going to be so upset when she hears."

Jules? She said it three times now. She always went by Julie.

"How could I forget? Stephanie never did make a play for Tim. She switched her attention to Jake because once I told her I would have liked to go out with Jake, she said she did too. And we both know how persuasive she was compared to me."

"Oh, Melody, we've come a long way from high school. You're no mashed potato now," Claire said. She picked up the wedding invite and dropped it back into her bag.

"Ha-ha. Yeah, I'm a French fry. Thanks, Claire. I'm sorry I'm so moody today. It's been a lot." I walked through the lobby and looked into the empty Rose Viewing Room with its tiny rose-clustered wallpaper and dark cherry woodwork. One of the crystal floor lamps was brightly lit, and the other lamp's bulb was flickering. "This place is making me feel claustrophobic. I shouldn't have come to work today. It's too depressing."

"Yeah, let's go. Someplace fun. This place gives me the creeps." Claire peered into the Rose Viewing Room and then started toward the door. "I don't know how you work here every day."

My cellphone began to ring.

"Wait, Claire. Mr. Snugg is calling me." I rushed back to my office and put my phone on speaker.

"Hello," Snugg said in the hushed voice he uses in the funeral home.

Claire stopped reading the "How to Keep Your Plants Alive in a Dead Growing Zone" brochure and ran over to listen in.

"Speak up, Snugg. You won't wake the dead," she whispered in my ear.

I quickly took the phone off speaker and motioned towards my spare office chair.

"Melody, Russell seems to think Ms. Gregor may have encountered foul play," Arthur Snugg said.

"What?" What kind of foul play?"

"Nothing for you to worry about, Melody. The police are handling everything. I am simply calling to check on you. I was a little gruff yesterday. Receiving that phone call was quite a shock."

"Mr. Snugg, she had an appointment with me. She collapsed in front of me."

"Unfortunately." Arthur Snugg loudly cleared his throat.

What did Stephanie say before she passed? It was so quick and shocking. Her speech was garbled and a whisper. I'm not sure.

"Melody, are you still there? Hang on. Alex, that is my lunch and my chips. Go buy your own," Snugg said sternly.

I walked from my office into the funeral home lobby. I began my usual pacing: ten steps toward the Lilac Room, turn, ten steps toward the Rose Room, and back around into the lobby.

"Mr. Snugg, if foul play was involved in her death, I don't like this."

In the background of Snugg's call, I could hear J.J. "Uncle A, they need your credit card for my lunch."

"I should have fought my divorce decree harder," Snugg said in a solemn tone. "Especially the part that said I had to employ Regina's nephews." Arthur Snugg sighed.

"Your ex did get the better part of that deal. But, Mr. Snugg, about Stephanie Gregor, did Russell tell you why he thinks it's foul play?" I stuck my hand into the dirt of the potted Peace Lily. It felt dry.

"Primarily her age and no underlying health conditions. They are running toxicology."

"When did he say this to you?" I took my phone away from my ear and checked it. No messages or missed calls from Russell. "He didn't call me!" I shouted as my hand squeezed one of the lily's leaves.

"Melody, please don't get upset. You did everything you could. It will be okay. I have to go. I'll talk to you on Monday."

The phone went dead. I opened the hall cupboard, removed my spray bottle, lightly misted the lily, and fluffed its leaves.

Russell thinks there was foul play in Stephanie's death, but he didn't tell me. Why? I thought we were partners in our relationship. I was the last one to see her alive…What if the perpetrator knew she came to see me? Could I be in danger now, too?

I went back to my office and quickly shut down my computer. Claire gave me two thumbs up.

"Let's get out of here, Claire." I hurried her through the lobby, pushed her out the funeral home door, and locked it.

"We can swing back and grab Blue Betty later," Claire said, looking up toward the bright blue sky and walking toward her white Camaro. "We need a road trip."

"Claire," I said, turning instead toward my Jeep. "I think I better go to the police station and talk to Russell."

"Okay, if you insist, but I am coming along. You need me today." Claire climbed into Blue Betty's passenger seat and buckled her belt.

"I'm glad you're my ride or die, Claire." I jumped on the driver's side and started my Jeep. "Although I don't plan on either of us dying anytime soon."

Claire turned up the radio, and I reached over and turned it off.

"I need to call Russell."

"Hey, Mel, I'm just on my way out the door on a call," he said, answering on the first ring.

"Russell, Mr. Snugg told me you suspect Stephanie was murdered! Why didn't you call me?"

"Boy, that didn't take long." Russell's voice was light, but he hesitated as he spoke.

"What do you think happened, Russell? Do you have any details?" Claire asked.

"You didn't say anything to me. Why? What happened? Do you know yet?" I put Blue Betty into drive but kept my foot on the brake. My hands gripped the wheel tightly as I waited for Russell's answer.

"Toxicology isn't back." Russell cleared his throat. "It might take a week or more."

"But you do suspect something?" I asked.

"She is our age, and from what we know so far, she had no other health problems. So yes, Mel, it's suspicious. Arthur took me saying suspicious and toxicology out of context. I wouldn't use the words 'foul play' just yet. I didn't say anything because we have to investigate."

"Russell, we know she wanted to talk to me. She had an appointment with me."

"It's going to be okay, Mel," Russell said.

"I wish everyone would quit telling me it's going to be okay!" I grumbled.

My phone beeped.

"My mother is calling." I sighed.

"It's okay, Mel. Oops. Listen, it's crazy here today; must have been a full moon. I can hear Claire in the background. Why don't you guys go do something fun? I will see you later tonight. We're still on for dinner and dancing at *The Artisan*, right?" he asked.

"Yes."

"Good, because I've been practicing a new dance move."

I'm hoping I'm in the mood to even go and dance. My mind is in overdrive, and I can't help but feel somebody did something to Stephanie.

"Mel? Are you still there?" Russell asked.

"Yeah, I'm sorry. And I'm sorry I snapped at you. It's just been a lot."

"Totally understandable," Russell said softly. "Listen, I'll see you later." He made what I hoped was a kiss noise and hung up.

I looked down at the missed call from my mother and then out at the road ahead. I put my phone in the console, turned the radio up loud, and stepped hard on the gas pedal.

The sun beat down, warming me, Claire, and my Jeep, Blue Betty, as I drove down Route 50 and then took the Admiral Street exit. Up ahead, I saw the sign for the Admiral Hotel, the upcoming wedding spot. I turned into the parking lot.

"This is the hotel for the wedding," I said as I swiveled in my seat to face Claire.

"Let's go. We've got to check this out." Claire cast her glance toward the hotel and tilted her head in an onward motion. "I heard this hotel is going to get a major renovation. Maybe part of that revitalization project to help out the small towns and businesses along Route 50."

The lobby of the Admiral Hotel was elaborately decorated in a ship's theme.

"Pretty odd and old looking, but how appropriate for Rachel and Brandon. He was the VP of the sailing club," I said, looking around at the sails hanging from the ceiling and the wooden walls.

"Yeah, looks like they started the renovations already. All these sheets hanging around." Claire pointed toward the reception area.

"I'm pretty sure those are supposed to be sails." I lightly nudged my friend with my elbow.

"Remember that sailing club sprang into place when Tim McCoy's dad donated two Sunfish boats and an FJ for use out on Pleasantview Lake." Claire rubbed her thumb and finger together. "Money."

Tim McCoy was a soft-spoken, nose in a book and eyes peering over the book at all the girls kind of guy. His dad was Pleasantview Trust's bank manager. They lived in the largest house in our small town.

"I think his dad thought the club would help him fit in," I said.

"He didn't know his son very well." Claire snorted.

We approached the reception desk where a middle-aged woman sat dressed in sailor attire.

"Their marketing department takes the Admiral idea to extremes," I whispered to Claire.

"I would have never guessed," Claire whispered back.

"Yo Ho Ho!" I said in my best pirate voice when we reached the plank-topped check-in desk.

The woman's eyes glanced up from her computer screen. Her mouth set in a downward frown. "What can I do to help make your day sail along?"

"Tired of the whole sailor's façade," Claire said exuberantly.

"We are stopping by as we have a wedding here and wanted to check out the room. We are in charge of centerpieces and the balloon arch." The words flowed effortlessly out of my mouth as if they were true.

As if mocking me, a large sail display next to the receptionist flapped loudly. She reached over and spun the knob on a portable fan to off.

"That took the wind out of the sails," I said.

Claire and I both snickered. The woman did not.

"Which room are you in?" she asked.

"I'm not sure. The wedding is next Saturday, at 7:00 p.m. Did you bring the invite in, Claire?"

Claire began to dig through her purse. The receptionist's scowl deepened as she checked her computer screen.

"You are in the Scuttlebutt Room, down the hall to your right." She picked up a piece of paper and began to read, "Please don't arrive to decorate until after 2:00 p.m. that day. The door to the room doesn't lock. Also, there is nothing to be attached to the walls, including your balloon archway, and please refrain from lighting the candles. They are decorative. If lit, they set off the sensitive sprinklers." She set down the paper and added, "Save the lighting of candles for your own home fires."

"Aye, aye," I said.

When she returned to staring at her computer, Claire and I headed down the hall to check out the Scuttlebutt.

"Looks like about 50 people tops," Claire said as we stood in the doorway looking into the room.

"Pretty close. The room is pretty tight, with eight tables in here, each with seating for six. Forty-eight chairs," I said quickly doing the easy math.

"I wonder if they'll postpone the wedding?" Claire said.

We walked into the room. Aside from the seating circling a small dance floor, two long, white folding tables were set up against one wall, and one tiny square table was positioned at the side. There was a small bar area with four bar stools in front. The counter held a working sink and a square napkin holder fixed to the countertop.

"It appears their napkin holders go AWOL frequently," I said, pulling on the napkin holder. "We might as well go, Claire. Thinking of a celebration now just doesn't seem right."

We turned to leave and I bumped right into a man hurrying into the room.

"Excuse me, I'm Morgan, the event coordinator. How can I help you?" He straightened his tie and beamed. He wore a captain's hat and white uniform complete with epaulets with anchors.

The hotel employee uniforms had to be an employer's cruel joke. I bit my lip to stop from laughing out loud. Claire grabbed hold of the napkin holder to steady herself. Her eyes were glazed over and she was staring. She wouldn't be making this man walk the plank. This was someone she wanted to be marooned with on an island.

Morgan was eye candy. What girl doesn't love a man in uniform? However, it was easy to get caught up in the moment, but laughable because his name tag said *Captain Morgan.*

I found my sea legs and spoke. "Ahoy, Matey. I'm Melody Shore, and this is Claire. We stopped by to look at the room for a party this coming Saturday. We are thinking centerpieces and balloon..." I stopped. I didn't know anything about balloon arches and didn't want to be questioned. "And maybe balloon animals," I said instead. I flashed my two-years of high school braces smile.

"I'll mark that down. There was a woman here already talking about renovations. I've been trying to phone her as this is my first event, and I want the bride and groom to sail into matrimony with no problems. I can't reach her, though. She doesn't answer her phone." He opened his clipboard-style binder, pulled out a paper, and attached it to the binder's front.

"Renovations? Do you mean decorations?" Claire asked with a silly smile on her face.

"Who would that be?" I asked, moving close to him and peering over his shoulder.

"Stephanie Gregor. I have been trying to call her since yesterday."

Claire and I gasped in unison.

"She's not available, but Claire is, " I said.

"Oh, good. Can you give me your input while you're here on the menu?" Morgan's hopeful bushy eyebrow raise caused Claire and me to sit down at one of the tables and motion for him to join us.

"The groom was here earlier, and I forgot to go over this with him. When I called, he and his wife-to-be seemed to be arguing. He shouted, 'You take care of it.' Then he hung up." Morgan's face flushed with color.

So, for the next 15 minutes, we discussed food and bar set-up times. I chose the medium-priced alcohol with the bar remaining open during dinner. I thought everyone would like that.

"I think that's about it then." Morgan picked up his white "Anchors Away" wedding folder and stood. The folder slipped from his hands, and as it fell to the table, a piece of blue flowered paper floated down to the floor.

I picked it up.

Claire and I both read it at the same time.

"B list."

There were two names on the "B list." Stephanie Gregor, and right below Stephanie's name, my name, Melody Shore.

Claire quickly straightened the folder and handed it back to Morgan. I shoved the page into my bag.

"Morgan, we appreciate your time, but we have to go now." Claire grabbed my arm and pulled me from the chair I was sitting in. After she propelled me out the door, she turned around and said, "Morgan, I, Claire, hope to see you again."

Claire speedily guided me out through the lobby and into the parking lot. She opened the driver's door to Blue Betty, gently pushed me in, and hurried into the passenger seat.

I found my voice once we were alone in my Jeep.

"Claire, I'm on the 'B list.' How? Why? That means I'm not invited unless someone drops out. How did you get invited, and I'm a 'B lister.' I picked the food and everything." I put Blue Betty into drive and sped out of the parking lot.

Neither Claire nor I spoke for the first five minutes I drove down Route 50 toward Pleasantview.

Claire loudly cleared her throat.

"This is crazy. The wedding is probably going to be canceled," she said.

"Cancelled? Why? Stephanie and I are, or I guess in her case, were, 'B-listers.'"

"I can't believe it. Like, why am I invited? I've spoken to Brandon and Rachel a handful of times since high school." Claire dug in her purse for her phone.

"You got me there. That's more than I have." I negotiated a sharp turn a little too quickly and Claire and I both swayed to the right.

"I hope Julie doesn't want to return the cocktail dress," she said, looking down at her phone. "Good, no messages. Before I stopped this morning to visit you, I spent all the money she paid me except $10 on these new boots from 'Boot Heaven.'" Claire lifted her leg to show off ankle-high, sapphire blue leather boots.

"Claire, I think we should go and talk to Brandon and Rachel. Do you know where they live?"

"Not in Pleasantview anymore, we know that. Last year at the reunion they said they own a bar. Hoff's Bar & Grill in Foxmoor. We need to go some time. You know what else, Julie told me she heard Tim McCoy's dad owns the Admiral Hotel, and Tim practically gave the use of the hotel to Brandon and Rachel for the wedding."

"Claire! Why didn't you tell me? We could have asked Morgan if Tim was there or if he worked there. He might know why Stephanie sought me out."

"I don't know. I wasn't thinking. That whole ship-themed hotel threw me. If it weren't for the cutie wedding coordinator." Claire pulled out her compact mirror and reapplied her lip gloss. "I don't mind asking Morgan about Tim. I'll just call the receptionist and ask for him."

"I think we should go back." I slowed Blue Betty down and pulled into an empty strip of storefronts. "Why did Stephanie go to the hotel if she was a 'B lister' too? And why did she have an invite?"

"The whole thing doesn't make sense," Claire said, shaking her head and holding her finger over her phone ready to dial.

"Even though I'm not invited to their wedding, I still think we have to go tell Brandon and Rachel that Stephanie is gone so they know. Their wedding is in seven days."

Claire looked down at her phone again and then at the clock on the dashboard.

"Shoot, Melody, I can't go. Besides, I'm sure they know by now. I have to be back at the store."

"Another date with Julie?" I asked, not doing a good job of hiding my third-wheel jealousy of Claire's rekindled friendship.

"No. Well, sort of. She said she would be stopping later." Claire reached across the Jeep and touched my arm. "I need to be back at the store to finish inventory. I was going to go through everything and see what I have to wear to the wedding. I'll look for a few outfits for you to try too."

"Claire! I'm not even invited. I'm on the 'B list.' I bet that invite was Stephanie's. Someone had RSVP'd no and she was now invited."

"With her dying, that moves you up the list."

"Claire!"

"I'm sorry. That was horrible for me to say."

"It doesn't make sense. What would be so important that she would make an appointment? Why not pop in? I wish I could remember what she said to me before she passed. It almost sounded like she was trying to warn me, like she was in danger. Oh, Claire, if we find out foul play was involved, why and who? And, am I next?"

"Melody, you are way ahead of yourself."

"Maybe 'B list' doesn't really stand for what we think. What if it's a hit list and I'm truly next? What if it's the business list, like take care of business, or blow, like blow them away? There's also blackmail, bribery, and bloodshed. They all start with B." I stepped down hard on the gas pedal.

"You're losing it. I know you are very intuitive and have great investigative skills, but I don't think foul play is involved." Claire checked her seatbelt and moved her arms to brace herself on the dashboard.

I slowed down from 55 miles per hour to the road's speed limit of 35.

We continued the rest of the return trip in silence until we pulled into the Peaceful Rest. Claire swiveled in her seat and touched my arm again.

"Look, don't do anything crazy. Why don't you stop by the store tonight and see Julie? She will be so excited to see you."

"Yeah, especially since she won't get to talk to me at the wedding."

Claire sighed loudly. "Come by. Please." She jumped out of Blue Betty and headed toward her white Camaro.

I can't go to Claire's store to reminisce with her and Julie and grieve over Stephanie's passing. Russell and I have a date tonight. With what just happened at the hotel, I almost forgot.

Claire waved and pulled out of the parking lot. When she was out of sight, I phoned my mom.

"Melody, I haven't heard from you in days. I stopped at your apartment today. You didn't get the deadbolt on your door yet that we talked about."

"Hello to you too, Mom. I've been a little busy, and it hasn't even been 48 hours since we talked." I exhaled loudly.

"Melody, have you been eating? I can make more tuna noodle. Tuna was on sale at *Shop Right*. I bought a case." I could hear my mom opening kitchen cupboards as she spoke.

"Why wouldn't I be eating?" I considered faking a bad connection and hanging up. But I forged ahead. "Mom, do you still talk to Mrs. Grey?"

"That horrible woman. No. She turned the whole book club on me. Just because I didn't read her month's selection and spilled a little red wine on her new white carpet. The wine was barely chilled."

"Mom, you never read any of the books, and it depends on the type of wine. Oh, never mind. Do you think she got upset because you told her she has horrible taste in reading?"

"Ha. I just think everyone could learn a lot from gossip magazines and self-help books."

"Speaking of books, Mom, do you have any on weddings? Like when you invite the B list people and who should be on it?"

For a brief second, there was silence over the phone.

"Do you remember your Aunt Sue, your dad's sister? I was on the B list for her bachelorette party. That woman was such a bore. She sure was glad though when one of her eight bridesmaids couldn't make it, and your dad told her I was available. I'm always the life of the party."

"Mom, did you go out with friends once you and Dad became serious?"

"Melody, is Russell treating you okay?"

"Yes, Mom, he's wonderful. I was thinking more about how time and distance change people."

"Well, yes, dear. I have wonderful books on things like that. I also have books on 'the change,' but you are too young for that. I think. You are feeling okay though, aren't you? You go to the doctor regularly. No hot flashes, night sweats?"

"Mom, everything is great. I was just looking for some new reading."

"Of course. I will drop some off later tonight."

In the background of the call, I could hear a loud beeping.

"Can you bring them on Monday to The Peaceful Rest? I'm going out tonight with Russell."

The last thing I want is for my mother to be the third person on my date.

"Sure, dear, if you don't need them right away. I am going to go now. My oven timer just dinged, and I want to get my buns out of the oven before they burn."

I hung up with my mom, turned Blue Betty's radio up a few notches, and did a search for the address of Hoff's Bar & Grill.

Hoff's Bar & Grill sat on the outskirts of the cultural district in the neighboring town of Foxmoor. Foxmoor is about fifteen minutes from Pleasantview and filled with big, old, foursquare homes. I hadn't been there since I went to visit Frances Blooming. Frances was the former owner of *Cash for Golden Treasures*. A woman with a true heart of gold, and the reason I met Russell. He was working undercover on a stakeout at her house and we met when jewels were missing from one of our deceased at the funeral home. Frances and I did hot yoga together and she is the reason I now own Blue Betty, my first vehicle with less than 80,000 miles.

A large wooden sign welcomed me to Foxmoor; a quiet community, inhabited mostly by people with hefty bank accounts.

When I arrived at the cultural district, there wasn't much to see other than a movie house and several restaurants. Around a bend, down an alley, and next to a florist sat Hoff's Bar. The sign on the door read "No bathing suits." The menu tacked to a wooden board on the outside of the partial brick, partial wood building listed hamburgers, chicken wings, almost famous nachos and to attract the in-crowd, locally grown, sustainable, organic produce deep fried to perfection. My stomach growled in approval. They had a selection of two domestic beers on tap, and one seasonal craft and import were available.

The inside was slightly nicer. There were booths lining the walls and four smaller high-top tables positioned to the left of the large, wooden step-up bar area. A high-tech dartboard hung on the back wall. Several men sat at the bar, engrossed in a sports TV broadcast of baseball. They turned and gave me the once over when I entered.

Brandon Hoff was leaning against the far end of the bar. He was still the thin-framed, tall guy with a killer smile I remembered. His dark brown hair had lightened and receded slightly from his forehead.

Rachel had her back to me but I immediately recognized her red hair pulled up in a ponytail. She still had a very petite figure. She slammed the cash register drawer and turned to Brandon.

"Don't try to smooth talk your way out of this. You couldn't do it, so I had to," she said.

"I tried, but you know how she can be. Um, Rachel, turn around and look who just came in the door."

Brandon smiled, wiped his hands on a towel, and began to move around his fiancée toward me.

"None of this would have happened if you and Tim…" Rachel stopped mid-sentence and spun around. She reached out and pulled Brandon to an abrupt halt.

"I'll be downstairs, the cases need stacking," he said, quickly pivoting around the bar and hurrying toward a set of stairs.

"Melody Shore," Rachel said, coming from behind the counter. She hugged me. "It's so wonderful to see you. You came to Foxmoor. To our bar. I'm shocked." She took a step backward.

Why did I come here? I'm not even invited to their wedding.

I cleared my throat and forged ahead. "Well, first of all, Rachel, congratulations on your upcoming wedding."

"Thanks. We've been so busy that we haven't had time to..." Rachel gave me a tight-lipped half-smile. "It's a small wedding, having some friends there will be nice."

"I bet," I said loudly. "B list," I muttered under my breath. I picked up a bar napkin and pretended I was interested in the logo on it that read Hoffs in calligraphy.

"What did you say?" Rachel said moving close again.

"Nothing. I'm sure the wedding will be wonderful."

"Oh, thank you. It's great you stopped in." She looked around her mostly empty bar. "We don't technically open until 4:00. I can make you a drink, though."

"No, that's…, you know what, I will have a drink."

"Great. What's your poison?" she asked, walking back behind the bar.

"Huh?" I could feel a cold sweat running down my back.

"You know, what do you want to drink? No charge." She motioned at the alcohol lining the wall behind her.

"Oh, give me whatever you have on draft. Not light." I pointed at the taps.

She pulled a beer glass from under the bar and poured me a drink. After I took three long sips, savoring the crisp, smooth taste, I spoke.

"I have bad news. I'm just going to come out and say it. Stephanie Gregor is gone."

"Gone. Gone where?"

"You didn't know? She's dead. I wanted to come in person to tell you." I brought the beer glass again up to my lips, but didn't drink.

Rachel stopped wiping down the bar and focused her eyes on mine.

"What do you mean, gone? Dead? I thought…Is this supposed to be a joke?" she asked, leaning forward over the bar, her face out of focus through the beveled beer glass.

"It's the truth, Rachel," I said, setting the glass down on the Hoff napkin.

"Brandon," Rachel screamed.

Brandon jogged up the steps. He stopped when he reached the top and looked hesitantly back and forth from his bride-to-be and me.

Rachel threw her bar towel down and ran towards Brandon. However, he wasn't waiting with open arms like the scene in *Dirty Dancing*. She collided into him, full force. Luckily, Brandon reached out and braced himself on the door frame, saving them both from toppling down the steps, and me once again having to call the EMS.

"Stephanie is dead, Brandon. Dead. She's dead," Rachel shouted.

"What?" Brandon looked down at his fiancée and then zeroed his eyes on me.

"It's true. The police are investigating, and I'm sure they will find out if foul play is involved." I reached into my purse and felt around for my phone.

I must have left it in Blue Betty's console. I'm trapped with no communication.

The future newlyweds locked eyes and together walked to stand on either side of me. My hand tightly gripped the beer glass.

"Melody, you said Stephanie. Stephanie Gregor?"

"Yes, Brandon."

"How did she die? Do you know?" he asked.

"You said foul play. Why did you say foul play? Are police involved? Do they suspect something?" Rachel added in one breath.

"Everyone calm down. Melody, let me get you a drink. I got just the thing for you," Brandon said, taking my beer from my hand and swiftly dumping it in his sink.

A different drink. I haven't even finished my beer. I should never have come here without telling Russell or bringing Claire. Slow down...I'm being ridiculous. Why would a bride and groom, old friends, hurt a "B list" invitee? But, since I told them, their mannerisms and questions are not what I expected, and it's making me very suspicious. I can't help but think they were arguing about something or someone when I walked in.

"No. I'm good. I stopped because I thought you would want to know about Stephanie. I'm sorry to break the news right before your wedding. That's all. Oh, look at the time." I looked down at my butterfly watch. "I've got to go. Thanks for the beer." I hurried out of the bar. When I turned around to see if anyone was following me, I could see Brandon standing in the doorway to Hoff's. Once back in Blue Betty, I pressed my door lock button and quickly drove away.

I arrived home and hurriedly changed into the coral, sleeveless, A-line dress. Next, I pulled my hair up in a messy but sexy, loose bun, freshened my makeup, and applied gold eyeliner and pink desire lipstick. I smiled in the mirror. I was ready.

Ten minutes later, Russell arrived. He gave me a passionate kiss and then held open the door of his blue Ford F-150. He tuned the radio to a station playing love songs and we drove to *The Artisan* with him at the wheel and me cradled against his shoulder.

The Artisan is a restaurant at the top of a hill overlooking Pleasantview. It used to be called *The Mountain.* The new owners retained the wood beams, hardwood floors, and leather booths. My mother said they hired a decorator who revamped the hometown ambiance by creating an eclectic vibe eatery showcasing the works of Pennsylvania artists.

Russell read the specials out loud from the large wooden chalkboard easel as I admired the art-adorned walls.

"I'm getting the prime rib." He rubbed his flat abs in approval. "They have your favorite on special tonight, the strawberry, almond, salmon salad."

I walked along the waiting area hallway lined with artwork.

"There's a real mishmash of art here, as my mother would say." Above me hung a black and gold painting of football players, a watercolor landscape, and next to that art, a distorted face-shaped wall planter with succulents protruding from the top where the hair would be. Across from the planter was a metal tree with branches shaped into a heart. Each leaf and bird on the tree was individually painted.

"Do you think the artwork gives the place a cozy and inviting feel?" Russell asked, coming over and taking my hand in his.

"It's different." I glanced back at the face-shaped wall planter and leaned in for a kiss.

After the hostess seated us and the waitstaff brought out a bottle of Pinot Grigio wine and a plate of bruschetta and calamari appetizers, I told Russell that I had found out that Stephanie and I were "B listers" for the wedding.

"What is a 'B lister?'" Russell asked, his voice morphing into police questioning mode.

"It's someone who isn't invited unless others cancel. Boy, this calamari is good."

"How did you find that out?" Russell reached for my hand as I went to pick up another calamari.

"Well, when you told Claire and me to go do something fun, we took a ride." I dropped his hand, quickly picked up the calamari, and popped it into my mouth.

"And?" Russell leaned forward.

"We drove to the Admiral Hotel."

"Did they have a posted guest list? Or a posted 'B list?'" Russell asked, his forehead wrinkled in confusion.

"No. But, Stephanie had been there on Thursday. The day before she came to see me."

"The hotel told you this?" Russell's beautiful brown eyes narrowed.

"Claire and I got to talking with Morgan, the event coordinator. Claire thinks he's cute and has her eyes on him. He told us Stephanie had been there and he had the 'B list' in his paperwork." I made air quotes with my hands when I said "B."

"Why would you be looking at his paperwork?"

"After we helped him with some last-minute wedding coordinator decisions, it dropped from his folder." I picked up my wine glass and took a drink.

"Slow down, Mel. Let me get this straight. You aren't invited to the wedding, but you helped with decisions, and then the 'B list' just fell out of the folder."

"Yeah, can you believe it?"

"Actually no, but, okay. Who else was on the list?" Russell held up his finger to tell me to wait to respond as he turned and motioned to the waitstaff.

"Can I borrow a pen?"

He unwrinkled his drink napkin, readied his borrowed pen, and nodded his head.

"You really are a cop." I sighed.

"Sorry, I didn't bring my field book. This sounds crazy, but it might help me. If you don't mind telling me who all was on this list?" Russell's deep brown eyes gazed into mine.

"That's what's strange. Only Stephanie and me." I cleared my throat.

"I guess I don't need the pen." Russell clicked the pen off and laid it back on the edge of our table. "Okay, Mel, after you saw a list with your and Stephanie Gregor's name on it, what did you do?"

"Well, Claire and I were shocked. We sort of left. Claire went back to her store to meet with Julie and I drove to Brandon & Rachel's bar."

"Okay, slow down again. You went to the bride and groom's bar. Why? And, who is Julie?"

"She's another friend from high school who is in town for the wedding. It seems she and Claire are on the invite list. I went to the bar to tell Brandon and Rachel about Stephanie. Are you investigating them? If not, you should be."

"Why would you think the bride and groom would be involved?" Russell put his hand back on top of mine.

"They were acting really suspicious when I showed up and told them that Stephanie had passed away." I squeezed his hand.

"Maybe they were in shock."

"To see me or to hear about Stephanie?" I let go of his hand and took a swig of my wine.

"Mel, let's not jump to conclusions. Who is Julie again?" Russell finished the calamari and wiped his mouth with his napkin.

"An old friend from school, but if you want to know about her, you should ask Claire. They are becoming really chummy." I downed my wine. "I hope the band starts soon."

"Me too." Russell took a sip from his glass. "Okay, it sounds like I will need to talk to Claire to get Julie's info. I'm sorry about everything you are going through. First Stephanie, and then this whole not-invited thing."

"Yeah. Rachel acted so smug. A small wedding with friends. What am I? I know those two are up to something. I need to find out what." I picked up the wine bottle and poured myself another glass.

Russell's leg started to shake. Russell and I have never had a big fight. We have had several minor tiffs which usually start because of my excessive curiosity. I could tell from his widened eyes, pierced lips, and bouncing leg that he was upset because I was. He leaned toward me.

"Mel, I know you want to know why Stephanie Gregor came to see you, and it was horrible that she passed away in front of you, but please, leave her death investigation to my department. Okay?"

"Russell, you know I need to know why she came to see me. Who are you investigating? Are the Hoffs on the list?"

"Mel, you know I can't disclose information about an investigation."

Our delicious dinner did nothing to lighten the new atmosphere at our table for two. And to add to it, when the band started, they were playing Russell's least favorite music, punk rock. We danced a few songs and came back to the table.

"I have to work tomorrow morning," Russell said when we sat down. "Would you mind if we called it an early night?" He yawned and covered his mouth with his hand.

"Yes. No, it's fine. I'm tired too."

I was home by 10:00 p.m. I tried to call Claire and when she didn't pick up, I went to bed. My dreams of having a wonderful evening were squashed. Instead, I spent the night in a restless sleep, dreaming of Stephanie and waking in fits of panic that foul play was involved in her death and she was trying to warn me.

I got up unusually early at 7:00 a.m. on Sunday. Over coffee at my kitchen table, I did a little address internet searching on my laptop. My cat, Shady, sat at my feet dressed in his breakaway, blue and black bowtie collar. I bought it to match my favorite striped flannel shirt of Russell's. Shady was purring loudly, oblivious to the goings on in my world.

After my coffee and a fast shower, I opened my closet to see what I could wear for the day. I decided overnight that I would do a little investigating of my own into Stephanie, and it wouldn't hurt to wear a disguise just in case. My wardrobe mainly consisted of beautiful swing dresses and pencil skirts. In the back of the closet, I found what I was looking for. My Halloween costume from two years ago. A courier outfit. I added a brown, crossbody satchel bag to complete my look. The bag would serve a dual purpose. I could carry my wallet, keys, and notepad easily, and the satchel's wide strap would hide the nacho cheese stain that I was almost able to remove from the front of my courier shirt. I finished dressing and was twirling in the brown flare skirt in front of my full-length mirror when I heard a loud knock at my door.

How am I going to explain this to Russell? Maybe I can gloss it over.

I fluffed up my hair, applied lip gloss, and looked out the front window for Russell's F-150.

Parked in my driveway was a Ford, but not Russell's. It was my mom's red Ford Focus.

When I didn't open the door quickly enough, she used her key and walked in. She carried two casserole containers. One marked tuna noodle and through the clear lid of the other, I could see a large stack of Russell and my favorite Sunday brunchtime treat, Palacsinta or Hungarian pancakes.

"Did you use Gram's recipe?" I asked as I opened the lid and reached for a powdered sugar Palacsinta.

"Your father and I used to role play," my mother said turning and putting the containers down on my table and looking me up and down from head to toe.

I could feel the heat rising up my neck. I opened the refrigerator and leaned in for a minute. Then, I put the containers in, poured my mom a cup of coffee, and sat down at my kitchen table with her.

"I thought you might want the books today, so I brought them, dear." She opened up her bag that is embossed with "Bingo is my Sport" and handed me two self-help books - "Even if You Aren't Invited, Go Anyway," and "The Shiniest Apples Could Still Be Rotten."

"Thanks, Mom." I put the books on my counter. "I need to ask you a question."

"Sure, anything, dear." My mother took my hands in hers.

"Do you remember Stephanie Gregor?"

"Of course, dear. How is Stephanie?" My mother squeezed my hands.

"Ouch." I pulled my hands away and told my mom what had occurred on Friday.

"That's horrible, but so nice of you to try to save her." My mother patted my arm and then stood up. "I can't believe I didn't hear anything. Of course, when her mother passed away, her father didn't want to remain friends. He hasn't returned any of my calls in years."

"Mom, they were divorced for years, and he moved out of town. You told me it wasn't a nice split."

"Well, yes, but he could have kept in touch." She sighed loudly.

I got up and took a Hungarian pancake out of the refrigerator.

"I better call Marsha and my church group members. They will need to know," my mother said, switching to reporter mode. She sat back down, removed her cell phone from her bag, and began to dial.

I quickly ate the pancake, grabbed the phone from her hand, and hit cancel.

"Listen, Mom, I have a few things I need to do today, so could you please call your best friend and the other ladies later?" I smiled at my mother.

"Sure, dear." She took the phone back from my hand.

"Before you go, do you know where Stephanie was living?" I subtly guided her to her feet.

"Of course I do. I know because Shirley used to live next door at 112, and I would see Stephanie when I went over to play *Just Dance* on that Wii game. Boy, I miss Shirley. That was great exercise. She moved over to Foxmoor." She swiftly produced a pen and paper from her bag and wrote the address for me as her rambling continued. "She lives in those duplexes on Woods Run. Her address is 111."

I gently nudged my mother closer to the door.

Should I tell her that Stephanie and I were on the "B list" for Brandon and Rachel's wedding? No, telling my mother and asking her not to say anything is equivalent to broadcasting it on national TV. She'd definitely pay a visit to Mrs. Hoff, and then there might be more than wine spilled.

Once my mom left, I waited until her car was out of sight before I headed out the door to investigate Stephanie.

I climbed into Blue Betty and tuned the radio to easy listening music, hoping the background acoustics would stop my mind from racing. I wanted to see where Stephanie lived and get a feel for who she had become. *Maybe one of her relatives will be at her house and I can speak to them.* My GPS gave me an ETA of thirty-seven minutes to her home. I drove out of Pleasantview heading west down Route 50 until I again reached Foxmoor. As I drove through the town, I looked out the window at the large homes, circular concrete driveways, and tree-lined streets.

I turned onto Woods Run. It was a steep hill with varying colors of aluminum-sided, two-story duplexes along the street. Each building had white shutter-framed windows. Halfway up the hill, I spotted 111. Stephanie lived in a Sandstone colored duplex. I parked across the street, facing up the hill, but then worried about gravity and whether my neighbor mechanic had actually fixed my parking brake this time. I pulled two bricks from the back floor of Blue Betty and wedged them against my tires. When Russell first saw the four bricks in my Jeep (because I carry enough to accommodate every hill size), he said, "Mel, most people carry jumper cables."

I climbed the twenty-two steps to the door of her duplex, thankful that I had gone for comfortable athletic shoes to match my courier outfit instead of my favorite brogues.

I rang the bell next to her red-painted door and waited.

No one answered Stephanie's door, but a gray-haired woman dressed in a purple velvet jogging suit stepped out of the duplex my mom's friend, Shirley, used to live in.

"Mail on a Sunday. Do you have anything for me?" She leaned over to peer into my bag.

"Actually, no. I'm here because I have a pick-up at this house." I secured my bag firmly under my arm. "Do you know the woman who lives here?"

The neighbor didn't answer. She started down the steps. When she was three steps down, she pivoted back around.

"Wait a minute," she said.

I could feel heat rising again up my face.

"I have some mail that was delivered to me by mistake." She pointed at Stephanie's duplex. "Since you're here, you give it to her."

She hurried up the steps into her duplex and came out with three pieces of mail. She thrust them at me and turned to leave.

"This is such a great neighborhood," I said, stepping in front of her.

"Yes, it is." She spun around and looked admiringly toward her front door and perfectly landscaped yard.

"I bet it's nice to have a good neighbor right next door."

She turned towards Stephanie's duplex and scowled.

"I can't help but notice that look. I take it you don't get along?" I walked closer and gave her an encouraging smile.

"My choral group tells me I don't have a poker face." She grimaced. "If they don't want me to lead practice and sound like a bunch of howling cats, let them. I don't."

Boy, this woman and my mother could be besties.

"So you and your neighbor don't get along?"

"Oh, we got along just fine until she wanted to redo my apartment, and I said no." She let out a huff noise.

"Redo it? What do you mean?"

"She used to sell life insurance, and then she took some online decorating classes, and now she's a decorator or thinks she is. I told her I'm on a budget and not interested. My decorating is just fine. She kept pushing it."

"That's not cool. I mean to push something on you." I looked toward Stephanie's duplex and shook my head.

"Exactly. I'm on a fixed income. She had a gathering last week, and I wasn't invited. It was a bunch of young women anyway."

"How do you know who went to the party?"

"I saw them when I was headed out the door. I play racquetball every Thursday night in a league." She bounced back and forth from her left foot to her right and mimicked a racquet in her hands.

"You wouldn't remember by chance what the women looked like?"

"I certainly would. I may be older, but my memory is sharp." She pointed to her head. "But, why do you want to know?" She leaned toward me, pushed her glasses down, and peered above her circular, thin frames.

"Oh, no real reason. The name Stephanie Gregor sounds so familiar. I went to school with a Gregor, I was just wondering what her friends looked like." I backed up a few steps from her.

The neighbor gave me a puzzled look but answered.

"Sure. There were two women. A shorter woman, with red hair and a tall brunette." She checked her watch and muttered under her breath.

That sounds a lot like Rachel Grey, but who is the tall brunette?

"My hair appointment is shortly. The early bird gets the middle spot under the dryers." She bounded down the steps without another word.

I looked down at the mail the neighbor had handed me. All three pieces were addressed to Ms. Stephanie Gregor. Apparently, she hadn't married, or if she had, she hadn't changed her name. The first was a water bill, the second a sweepstakes entry saying Stephanie had won one of three top prizes, and the third piece of mail was from "Davis & Held's Pharmacy." It was a flyer about natural supplements to boost health and wellness in the daily grind. The back listed the pharmacists, Dave Davis and Lindsey Held.

Lindsey Held.

Right before I left Pittsburgh to move back home, my mom mentioned that one of my old friends was now a successful pharmacist. Lindsey Held. My mother was hoping that she could get her new, now-necessary, anxiety prescriptions from Lindsey cheaper. Her not-so-tactful way of letting me know that, in her mind, my personal life was making her take new meds.

Bingo, as my mom says. Lindsey Held was a tall brunette.

I think Russell would be proud of my investigative techniques. Now to find Stephanie's mailbox. Crap, there isn't any...there has to be.

Then, I saw it. At the street level, a mail station with small separate boxes, each requiring a key to open.

"Oh great!"

I can't walk into the police station and say here's Stephanie's mail, Russell. I know you are investigating, but I went to Stephanie's home, got her mail, and questioned her neighbor.

I peered through the open blinds of Stephanie's duplex. For an interior decorator, she decorated modern, but a little eccentric for my liking. Her living room wall had a mask wall planter similar to the one at *The Artisan,* except instead of succulents, Stephanie's had long ferns for hair. *So strange…are these creepy masks the latest thing in decorating*?

I could make out a dark brown leather couch and a white throw rug. A thought began creeping into my mind about her dying on the white rug. So much better for resale to expire on someone else's rug, but unfortunately, it was Arthur Snugg's red rug, and I was there.

As I turned to leave, my satchel got caught on Stephanie's door handle. When I pulled to free it, the door pulled forward and then swung open.

I date a police officer…in Russell's eyes, this would definitely be breaking and entering…well, not breaking, but definitely entering.

It had been two days since she had passed away. I know the Foxmoor and Pleasantview police are busy, but Russell had said there was an investigation. I was sure law enforcement would have locked up after themselves.

Someone else must have been in her apartment. But who and why?

Maybe a relative or friend forgot to lock the door.

"Hellooo."

The next thing I knew, I was standing in Stephanie's living room.

Stephanie's home was neat and organized. Everything looked in place. A copy of a travel magazine lay open on her hand-carved mahogany coffee table.

I wandered from the living room into the kitchen. On the counter was a French press coffee machine. I felt the side.

That's odd. It's still warm.

The only other thing on the counter was an address book. I laid Stephanie's mail on the counter and then began to leaf through the address book. Under "E" for Evans, I found Jake's name and address. I pulled a MAC machine receipt out of my wallet and quickly jotted down his info.

The first door down the short hallway was a bathroom. You can tell a lot about a person by their bathroom. Stephanie's was lavender with sage green accent rugs and towels. The faucet handles, door knobs, and towel rack were bronze. I opened her medicine cabinet. No prescription drugs. But she had twelve bottles of nail polish, including three from the Wild West collection. I've been searching for the latest color, Rodeo Rose.

No wonder I can't find it anywhere; Stephanie bought up every bottle.

I picked up one of the bottles and twirled it in my hands.

What am I doing? I better get out of here before the police show up and tonight's news headline reads "Courier found in bathroom holding nail polish. Arrested for putting mail in the home."

Before I left, I peered into one more room. A bedroom. It was in shambles. Drawers were opened, and clothes were tossed around.

Was Stephanie a messy dresser, or was someone else looking for something? Had they found what they were looking for?

I headed back to her living room, intent on leaving. As I took one more look around the room and at the strange wall planter, I noticed a piece of flowered paper sticking out from behind a couch cushion. It was similar to the "B list" paper that Claire and I saw at the hotel.

I picked up the paper. In neat, calligraphy-type writing, someone had written the phone number for The Peaceful Rest. Under it was my name, Melody Shore, underlined in red and circled in an abstract design. I gasped, pocketed the note, quickly locked the door, and left.

Back at Blue Betty, I walked to the rear of my Jeep and bent to pick up my bricks. The one that was behind the left tire was gone. I rushed to the other side and bent to look behind that tire. That brick was missing as well. I stood and looked up and down the street. It was quiet and deserted. I opened my Jeep's back door and counted my bricks. There were two.

I'm positive I put a brick under each tire. Kids? Or did someone see me go into Stephanie's duplex? Was it the person who caused harm to Stephanie, and now they know I am searching for answers?

A sudden chill came over me. I quickly jumped back into my Jeep, hit the door lock, and started her up. Then, I entered the address for Jake I had gotten from Stephanie's address book into my GPS. With a final look at her home, I bowed my head and whispered, "Stephanie, you came looking for me for a reason, and I vow, I will find out why. I, Melody Shore, am no mashed potato." *At least not when I am safely locked in Blue Betty, and she is running.*

Ten minutes later, I arrived at the address Stephanie had listed for Jake Evans. There had to be some mistake. Blue Betty and I were parked in front of a Presbyterian church in the middle of Foxmoor. The sandstone brick building had stained glass windows and a placard mounted next to the large red doors. The placard read, "All Welcome."

It was 1:15, and my stomach growled. It had been several hours since my cup of coffee and Palacsinta. Lucky for me, there was a "Heavenly Smoothies" next to the church.

After enjoying an "Immortality Orange" smoothie, I visited the church.

The office seemed like a good starting point for help, so I followed the sign directing me to it. When I arrived, a young man dressed in soccer attire sat counting and organizing checks and cash. He had several empty collection plates in front of him.

"Oh, hi. You must be new to the route. No one picks up on Sunday from us. I don't have any packages ready. Soccer game." He pointed down to his shirt. "I just got back a bit ago."

"Huh?" I looked down at my courier clothing. In the excitement of the last hour, I forgot I had it on.

"Oh, I'm not collecting. I was in the neighborhood and stopped in. Is Jake Evans around?" I adjusted my bag so the strap fully covered the cheese stain.

"You missed him and the pastor by about five minutes." He smiled up at me.

My smoothie cost me more than $3.50, it cost me a chance to ask Jake if he knew why Stephanie sought me out.

"Do you have a few minutes? I was hoping to ask you some questions." I sat down across from him.

"Ask away. We are always glad to welcome potential new members." He folded his hands in front of him. "Like I said, the pastor isn't here, but I'm a deacon." He straightened his back and squared his shoulders.

"Oh, I'm not here to join."

His shoulders drooped.

Although this would be a pretty church for Russell and me to get married in, and I'm sure my mom would approve.

"Jake is an old friend of mine, but we haven't talked in a long while. I didn't know he had become a pastor." I reached into my bag, my fingers curling around the MAC receipt.

"He hasn't. At least, I don't think so."

"Oh. I'm confused. My friend, Stephanie, had the church's address listed for him." I pulled the slip out of my bag and read the address out loud.

"That's the church address all right. But, I haven't met any parishioners named Stephanie. Although if she isn't in the young adult group I mentor and doesn't play on the church soccer team, I doubt I would." He laughed an easy, friendly laugh and continued, "I only met Jake last week. He and the pastor are friends, and he is staying at the church temporarily. Sorry, I can't be any more help. Perhaps come back tonight. We have an evening service at 7:00." He glanced toward the stacks of money and then the wall clock.

I thanked him for his time and left. He didn't know it, but he had been very helpful.

Returning to the main entrance, I saw the programs for the evening service printed and stacked neatly on an end pew at the rear of the sanctuary. I picked one up and glanced through it. The back page listed outreach ministry services offered through the church. Below that, it read:

Sunday 6:00 p.m. Contemporary service–Pastor Lenny Blane.

We're Getting ~~Married~~ Murdered

Jake Evans's high school best friend and our former classmate.

Suddenly, I was positive about where I was spending my Sunday evening.

When I arrived home, Russell's truck was parked in front of the grassy, one-acre lot bordering my landlord's property.

I pulled into the driveway, climbed the wooden steps to my apartment, and opened the door.

Russell's shoes lay neatly on my throw rug, and his keys on my kitchen table. He was sitting on my couch, eyes closed, feet propped up on the ottoman.

I sat down next to him and rubbed his hand.

"Mel, we need to have a serious talk." Russell stood up. "Wait a minute, why are you dressed as a delivery person?"

I reached into my satchel and fingered the paper I had taken from Stephanie's apartment.

I don't want to withhold anything from Russell. He is an officer of the law. But if I tell him where I was and show him the paper, our serious talk will take an entirely different turn. He already knows Stephanie had made an appointment with me. Snugg confirmed that.

"It's silly. I wanted to play a prank on Claire. She wasn't at her shop, though. Now, what do you want to talk about?" I stood and took both his hands in mine.

"You're biting your lip. Is there anything you want to tell me?" Russell's brown eyes fixated on mine.

"I went over to Stephanie Gregor's, and the door to her duplex was open." I took a deep breath.

"You did what? Mel?" Russell's voice rose two octaves, and he pulled his hands away from mine.

"I know, I shouldn't have. I didn't see any family or anyone. Well, other than her neighbor. Wait until you hear what she told me."

Russell got out his notepad, and I reiterated what the neighbor had told me about Stephanie's profession and how she had a party the night before she died and the two invitees were a redhead and a tall brunette.

"Do you think the redhead could be Rachel Grey?" I asked.

"Could be, but there are a lot of women with red hair," Russell said, his eyes now fixed on his notes.

"The brunette, the other one, might be my old friend, Lindsey Held. She owns a pharmacy. Have you talked to her yet?" I walked to the kitchen and removed the casserole containing my mom's tuna noodle.

"Do you want any?" I held the dish out towards Russell.

"No, thanks. Did you go and talk to your other old friend, Lindsey?" Russell asked, peering into my refrigerator and spotting the Palacsinta dish. He pointed to it.

"No. I…well, I went to see Jake Evans." I handed him a plate and the casserole containing the crepes.

"Jake Evans. Why does that name ring a bell?" Russell asked as he removed a crepe and sat down at my table.

"He's the guy I used to have a crush on in school." I put the tuna noodle back in the refrigerator.

Russell ate the crepe, closed his notebook, and looked up at me.

"Mel, I know I am busy, but visiting old boyfriends?" He raised his eyebrows and pursed his lips.

"It's not what you think. I need to find out why Stephanie came to see me."

"And knowing you, you won't stop until you do. Now, is there anything else?" Russell asked.

"Oh, I almost forgot. I locked Stephanie's door."

Russell's phone buzzed. He checked it, groaned, and said, "I have to go." He placed his plate in my sink, picked up his keys, slid on his shoes, and left without our usual goodbye.

For a few moments, I stood staring out the window at him as he walked to his car. Then I called Claire.

"Hey, Melody," Claire said, picking up on the first ring. "I was going to call you. Russell called me today to ask questions about Julie. He is worried about you, and so am I."

"Russell was just here." I sat down hard on my wooden kitchen chair. "Claire, I called to see if you wanted to join me tonight at church." I took the church bulletin from my satchel and laid it on my table.

"Church? Um, is there a reason you want me to go to church with you? I mean, we used to go together as kids."

"I found out Lenny Blane is the pastor at a church over in Foxmoor, and when I went there today, I just missed Jake Evans." I opened my pantry door, took Shady's dry food from the lower shelf, and shook the container.

"Russell and I don't think you should be searching people down, but, oh, man, Jake Evans. Now I wish I had come along. How did he look? Good as ever?"

"Jake? I told you I didn't see him. I didn't see Lenny either." Shady magically appeared at the sound of the container opening and began to rub on my legs and parade around me, tail high in the air.

"So you are going to church twice in one day. Did you do something wrong that you aren't telling me?" Claire laughed a nervous laugh.

"Claire, you don't have to do something wrong to go to church, but I did just tell Russell I went to Stephanie Gregor's duplex."

"What? You went where? Melody, what is up with you?"

"I need to find out why Stephanie came to see me," I shouted. Shady skittered out of the room and then, being the ever-hungry cat he is, cautiously reappeared and reapproached his bowl.

"I know her death is really upsetting you, and being on the 'B list' for Rachel and Brandon's wedding doesn't help. Let me guess, you went to see Brandon and Rachel, too. Did you tell them about Stephanie, or did they know already?"

"Yeah, and they acted super suspicious." I moved over to the chair next to Shady and began to pet him as he happily munched his food.

"Suspicious? Like how?" Claire asked.

"When I told Rachel, she shrieked and ran into Brandon's unopened arms."

"Sounds like shock, not suspicious."

"You had to be there." I let out a loud sigh.

"Yeah, I guess. Maybe they were just upset because of the news, and also because there you were and they didn't ask you to their wedding."

"Could be, I guess. But I don't know. Oh, I didn't tell you yet, but I met Stephanie's neighbor, and she told me Stephanie threw a party last Thursday, and a redhead and a tall brunette attended." I began to rake my fingers through Shady's back fur. He arched his back but continued eating.

"You think the redhead is Rachel, don't you?" Claire asked.

"Claire, remember Lindsey Held?"

"Of course. But why are you bringing her up?"

"Claire! Tall brunette." My hand pounded down on my table, and Shady rushed behind the couch.

"Melody, these women were our friends. You surely don't think one of them hurt Stephanie."

"I don't know what to think, Claire. But it is suspicious. And, when I was in Stephanie's apartment, I found a note with my name on it."

"She did have an appointment with you. I'm sure she wrote it."

"Yeah, maybe. But this was neat handwriting. She always had sloppy writing."

"What did Russell say?"

"I didn't tell him about the note." I sighed.

"Melody! You better tell Russell and go to church."

"Thanks, Claire. Way to make me feel better."

After I hung up with Claire, I ate a piece of my mom's tuna noodle casserole. I was pleasantly surprised to find that she had added buttery breadcrumbs as I had requested on the last casserole drop-off. Then, I headed into my bedroom to change.

There had to be something in my closet appropriate for church and an impromptu meeting with a guy I had a crush on and hadn't seen in 10 years, and his best friend, who was now an ordained minister.

For my church attire, I decided on a yellow and blue flowered blouse and a bargain purchase from several years ago, a navy-blue swing skirt. I pulled my hair up and tied it loosely with a floral scarf.

At 5:45, the church lot held approximately twenty-five cars. I had to park in the last row.

"Hey, it's the delivery person. Glad you decided to come tonight," the guy from earlier said as I walked from the parking lot toward the church.

"Please, call me Melody."

Tonight, his soccer shirt and shorts were replaced by a light blue dress shirt, dark blue pants, and a red and blue striped bow tie.

"Wow, this church has a fantastic garden." I wandered toward the grassy back area of the church.

"Thanks," he said, smiling and running his hand through his dark black, wavy hair. "I didn't introduce myself earlier. I'm Ben, and I am really into plants. Got a green thumb, I guess." He held up both his thumbs for me to see.

"You're quite the gardener. The plant in the back over there, with the cascading white and pink flowers is beautiful. But, why is there a fence around it?" I asked.

"Brugmansia. Very beautiful, but also poisonous," Ben said.

The church bells began to chime.

"I've got to go, Melody. I'm the organist."

"Boy, you sure do a lot around here…wait a minute…Ben, why do you have poisonous plants at church?" A lump began to form in my throat.

"The others aren't harmful, Melody. Pastor Lenny planted that. He said he liked the name. He's not the gardener I am. I put a fence around it to keep animals out and admiring parishioners from touching it."

"This church is lucky to have you, Ben," I said.

Ben laughed and disappeared through a side door. I tried to follow.

"You can't get to the sanctuary that way. That's the office entrance." Stephanie's neighbor, the gray-haired, purple jogging suit woman, appeared next to me. Tonight she was dressed in a high collar, light purple, calf-length dress with matching shoes. She grabbed my arm and pulled me toward the main entrance. "This way," she said.

"I like what you did to your hair. It matches your dress and…" I looked towards her shoes as she sprinted us along. "I have never seen purple shoes like that."

"I wanted bright pink, but the hairdresser said purple is my color." She touched her purple-highlighted hair.

"Hi, welcome to Faith Church." A tall, bald gentleman wearing a dark blue sport jacket handed me a program. He nodded to the woman.

I mumbled "hello" and attempted to untangle myself from Stephanie's neighbor, who was still tightly gripping my arm. It was no use. She pulled me along to the front and settled us into the second row, pushing me in first and taking an aisle seat.

The church service was very inspirational, and our high school public speaking class had certainly paid off for Lenny.

"I see love all around us," Lenny said as he walked along the carpeted front of the sanctuary. "Love for our family, love for our friends. We show it in small ways and big ways. The way we help each other in times of need."

Tears welled up in my eyes as Lenny spoke.

"When I look out into today's congregation, I see your love for each other." Lenny's voice echoed in the quiet church. "And,…Melody Shore."

The notes Lenny was reading from fell to the ground. He quickly picked them up as Stephanie's neighbor rose and joined several parishioners at the front of the church. The choir began to sing the hymn "We Gather at the Altar" as the ushers walked up and down the aisles passing the collection plates.

Several times during the hymn, I caught Stephanie's neighbor rolling her eyes and abruptly turning toward the other choir members as their voices failed to harmonize, pitched, and squeaked.

She definitely doesn't have a poker face, and I have to agree with her, they could benefit from practice.

During the singing and offering, Lenny stood quietly at the pulpit, his hands gripping the sides. He looked downward and then back up. After glancing around the whole church, his eyes came to rest on me. I looked away to avoid direct eye contact and then turned around toward the churchgoers behind me. Most were softly chatting, looking down at their programs, or trying to quiet their children. I didn't see Jake or anyone else I recognized in the church.

After the hymn and collection, Stephanie's neighbor did not return to her seat. She and the rest of the choir exited down the left aisle and through a side door, arguing as they went. Lenny finished with a prayer, and then the church service concluded. As people began to leave, Lenny Blane hurried past several parishioners toward me.

"Melody Shore!"

"Lenny, it is so great to see you. Wonderful sermon."

"Thank you. What brings you to my church, Melody?" he asked.

"Well, to be honest, Lenny…I mean, Pastor Blane, I came here looking for Jake. I thought this was his address."

"Let's go to my office and talk." Lenny Blane looked squarely at me.

"Why do I feel like the bad kid in school? Wait, that wasn't me." I smiled up at him. "That was you, Lenny. Always cutting class and instead of studying during study hall, you spent your time charming the cafeteria workers for free food."

"What's not to like about study hall in the cafeteria? They always had extra. Why not share?" Lenny guided me down the hall to a door marked "Clergy."

"And, now, you're a minister. I've got to say I'm shocked."

We entered his office, and he motioned for me to sit in the chair opposite his desk. Then, he turned, removed his outer robe, and loosened his tie. He shut the door, but not before conspicuously looking up and down the hallway.

"Why are you looking for Jake?" he probed as he took a seat behind a large, dark walnut desk.

"Because of Stephanie Gregor. I wanted to ask him some questions."

I decided to slowly work into what I wanted to ask, an interview technique I had learned from watching *Murder She Wrote* with my mother.

I could hear a giant clap of thunder through the open window.

"Wow, some spring shower," I shouted as I sprang up from my seat.

Lenny got up and closed the open window in the nick of time before it blew his budding herb garden off the window ledge. The wind pushed the smell of rosemary and mint across the room.

"Did Stephanie tell you to contact Jake or me?" he asked, questioning in his dark green eyes.

"No. But I know about Rachel and Brandon's upcoming wedding this Saturday. Can I just ask you a few questions? I am interviewing some of the attendees of the party." I pulled a pen and notepad from my purse.

"Interviews? Of the attendees?"

"Yes, it might help me understand what is going on." I sat with my pen poised to write.

"What is going on, Melody?" he asked.

"Just a few questions, okay?"

Before he had time to protest, I started talking.

"Pastor Blane, a minister is quite an admirable career choice, and I'm sure very busy but rewarding when you can help others."

"Yes. My career choice keeps me rather busy." He reclined back in his chair.

"Do Jake or Stephanie attend church here?"

"Church, no. But I do see both of them." A confused look crossed his face.

"Is Jake here this evening? I didn't see him in church."

"No, he isn't. But, Melody, I thought you wanted to interview me?" He leaned forward and tried to look at my blank notepad.

I started throwing questions out like fastballs.

"Why would Jake have his address listed as the church?"

"Where is it listed?" Lenny asked.

"Ben told me he was staying here." *I don't like tossing Ben under the bus with his "boss," but I'm certainly not going to tell him I got the info from a deceased person's address book.*

"Lately, it's the easiest way to reach him," Lenny said in a matter-of-fact tone.

"Through you?

"Yes, Melody. Jake is sort of in between things."

"In between what sort of things?"

"What a minister and his friend discuss is private. What part of this interview pertains to me?"

"So you are still friends. Do you know why Stephanie would come to see me?"

"She came to see you?"

"Yes, and did you know now she's dead?" When I said it, my voice broke. I closed my notebook.

Lenny Blane bolted up in his chair.

"What? When?"

"On Friday. The police are investigating."

Lenny picked up his phone and scrolled through it. Then, he looked at me.

"On Friday I..." He cleared his throat and looked down. "take salsa dance lessons."

"Really!" I tried to hide my smirk as I pictured the six-foot Lenny Blane, dressed in his church robe, salsa dancing. "I wasn't asking where you were, Pastor Blane," I said.

"Of course you weren't. That's shocking about Stephanie. Do you know how she passed away?"

"No, but can you ask Jake to contact me?" I tore a piece of paper from my notebook, wrote the number of The Peaceful Rest down, and handed it to him.

"Lenny, do you keep in contact with any of the women from our old group?"

"Huh? Listen, Melody, I would like to stay and talk, but I have an appointment this evening and am running late. Now, if you will excuse me?" He stood and came around the other side of the desk, towering over me.

By the tone of his voice and his sullen eyes, I had worn out my welcome. He walked to the door and held it open without saying another word. Thrown out of a church by a salsa-dancing pastor. I can't even picture this happening to my mother.

The brief rain shower had stopped as quickly as it had started, and the evening sky glowed with hues of orange and red. The last of the parishioners were leaving the parking lot. I saw Ben in his car as I walked to Blue Betty, but there was no sign of Stephanie's neighbor. Ben waved as he pulled out onto the road. I had struck out finding Jake, and Lenny wasn't going to give him up to me.

When I arrived home, I sat at my table and wrote down my thoughts. Shady lay quietly on my feet.

1. Jake Evans – What's up with my old crush? I needed to ask him about Stephanie. Could he have done something, and is now hiding out at a church?

2. Rachel Grey and Brandon Hoff –The soon-to-be newlyweds didn't react the way I thought they would about Stephanie. They seemed nervous when I showed up at their bar. Was Rachel the redhead at the party? How many redheaded friends could Stephanie have?

3. Lenny Blane - I think this pastor knows more than what is written in the good book. How are Lenny and Jake connected now? He seemed shocked that Stephanie had passed away. Or was that an act? I can't picture him as a salsa dancer.

4. Lindsey Held –Is she going to the wedding? Claire didn't mention her, just Julie.

5.   Julie Paine – I need to make time to meet up with her.

6.   Tim McCoy – Does his dad really own the Admiral? From my research, I found out Tim owns an ice cream shop in St. Mare. Surely someone who dishes up ice cream would be sweet, and if he knew anything about Stephanie, he would tell me.

I tore the page from my notebook and then picked up the phone and called Russell.

"Hi, babe," he said when the call connected. "I'm sorry about before. The station is changing our computer system, and it has been nothing but trouble and a headache for me. I called you earlier, but you didn't pick up."

I doodled a heart on the paper as he spoke. Russell's voice was deep, with just the right amount of gravel.

"I went to church tonight." I looked down at my phone. I had silenced it during the service.

"Church. That's good. Taking a break from tracking down old friends and boyfriends."

"Actually, can you believe I ran into Jake Evans's best friend, and he didn't know Stephanie had passed away?" I picked up the list I had made, carefully folded it, and placed it in my paisley print work bag. Any word about the cause of Stephanie's death?"

"Melody, don't try and change the subject. How did you run into your crush's best friend? In church?"

"Yes. If you can believe it, the minister, Lenny Blane, is an alumnus of my high school."

"Let me guess, you asked him if he knew anything about Stephanie making an appointment to see you."

"Russell, I can't stop thinking about it. Did the toxicology come back yet?"

"Not yet, Mel." Russell sighed.

"This is horrible. She sought me out for a reason. When she came in the funeral home door, she said, 'I need help.' Then, when she collapsed, she said something like 'Someone…kill…me…Melody,' or something like that, her voice was faint." I got up from my computer desk and began to pace back and forth.

"She said what?" Russell's voice rose with each word.

"I'm not sure exactly what she said. I mean, it happened so quickly. You don't think I'm in danger, do you?" I sat down and began to rock in my desk chair.

"Mel, I wish you had told me all this sooner." Russell's voice was serious but turned consoling. "But, listen, let's not jump to conclusions. Let's wait for the toxicology report and focus on what we do know. Maybe she truly was stopping in to talk about the wedding with you. Maybe her dying has nothing to do with her making an appointment at the funeral home."

"Oh right, Russell," I said, my voice turning into a shriek. "I'm on the 'B list' and so was she. She seeks me out after 10 years and dies at my feet."

"Mel, I know this is upsetting."

"It's just that I've come to terms with my old career of working as a paralegal in Pittsburgh turning from a dream job into a life-crushing time when I was unjustly fired and my boyfriend cheated on me. But it brought me home. I would have never met you or reconnected with Claire."

"I can't imagine my life without you," Russell said softly. "And don't forget, you've become Arthur Snugg's right-hand woman. You've filled your dad's shoes pretty nicely. He would have been proud."

"Yeah, I know my dad used to be Snugg's right-hand man. That is until he passed away." I pulled a tissue from the nearby box and blew my nose.

"Mel, can you imagine Alex and J.J. without you there?" Russell chuckled.

"They do add laughter to my day. Living close to my mom, though, is something else, but at least I'm not living with her."

"Yeah, but you went and gave her your apartment key. Although I don't complain when there are casseroles stacked two high in your fridge."

"She finally found someone who likes her tuna noodle." I sighed heavily. "Boundaries are something my mother isn't good at."

"I also don't mind her six-pack of beer unannounced visits." Russell laughed heartily this time, and then his cop voice returned. "Back to my investigation of Stephanie Gregor's death. Is there anything else you left out?"

"Russell, I can tell you right now, Jake Evans, her high school boyfriend, is living at Lenny Blane's church, although he is MIA, and like I said, Lenny

Blane, his best friend in school, is a pastor now. He didn't know Stephanie had passed, and he takes salsa dance lessons."

"That's a lot, Mel. And the last comment…random."

All of a sudden, in the background of our call, I could hear a lot of noise.

"Great. One of the new computers just crashed again. I've got to go. Please don't go talking to old classmates. One of them could be the perpetrator and dangerous."

Perpetrator. Dangerous.

I pulled the list I had made back out of my work bag.

Tim McCoy, ice cream shop owner, and Lindsey Held, pharmacist.

How dangerous could getting ice cream and going to a pharmacy be?

Monday morning, I woke to Shady, sitting on my chest, staring into my eyes. He let out a loud distress meow when I tried to push him off and roll over. I rubbed my eyes, blinked, and focused on the clock. It was 7:50. In all the excitement of the past few days, I hadn't set my alarm for work, and Shady hadn't eaten in eight hours. Thank goodness for my cat's internal food clock. I quickly dressed in a pair of light blue, wide-legged capris and a blue and white polka-dot tank top with a white short jacket. For shoes, I chose a strappy, low, comfortable blue sandal. If I were going to visit my old friends after work, I wanted to look great but be able to move quickly should things escalate, and I need to make a speedy exit.

At the Peaceful Rest, things were back to normal. Arthur Snugg, Alex, and J.J. had returned from their weekend classes and were very pleased with themselves. Well, at least the twins were pleased.

"Check it out, Melody," Alex held up a paper certificate embossed with a gold seal.

"We passed!" J.J. chimed in.

"This class was a small step, but I am proud of you boys," Arthur Snugg said.

Alex patted J.J. on the back. J.J. returned the pat.

"You are making good on your promise to me last year of pursuing your mortuary science degrees." Snugg nodded at the twins, but then his voice turned gruff. "I will, however, be deducting from your salary the cost of the pool chairs that you broke in your chair stacking, pool diving escapade."

"We understand, Uncle Arthur," Alex and J.J. responded in unison.

"They just don't make wicker like they used to," J.J. added.

"Hey, Mel, you should have seen it. A guy in class passed out." Alex said, changing the subject.

J.J. faked falling to the floor, to which I let out a groan and shut my eyes.

"Didn't know he was allergic to menthol. It gets pretty smelly. We needed to apply menthol to our upper lips," J.J. piped in.

"I think it was the five beers he had Friday night at the pool that did him in," Alex added earnestly. "11:00 a.m. is too early for a Saturday autopsy class, even for us early risers." He patted his chest.

"Melody had a very stressful weekend. I told you boys that her friend passed away here. You two need to be more sensitive. Now, I know you have work to do." Arthur Snugg sternly pointed out the window toward the cemetery gardens.

"We are very sorry, Mel," Alex said.

J.J. hugged me, and then they turned in unison toward the lobby where Stephanie had fallen. With downcast eyes, the twins both nodded their heads and hurried toward the basement steps.

"I, too, am sorry about what happened to you on Friday, Melody." Snugg pursed his lips and raised his eyebrows. "Unfortunately, we see a lot of death in this job."

"Mr. Snugg, she was my age and passed away right in front of me." My eyes began to tear up. "Do you think she was allergic to something?"

"She could have been." Snugg gave me his consoling funeral director face and then said, "Melody, it was very thoughtless of me to say we see a lot of death." Arthur Snugg handed me a tissue. "If you need a few days off, I understand."

Snugg's flip phone began to play his ringtone, *Death in Paradise*. He pulled it out of his pocket, and his face lit up into a smile.

"Melody, if you're sure you're okay?" He gently patted my shoulder in a fatherly gesture.

"Yes, Mr. Snugg, please take your call." I wiped my eyes with the tissue and began to sort through the folders piled up on my desk for Monday's daily tasks.

Snugg hurried from my tiny office and up the mahogany staircase to his large, swanky office, cooing into his phone with each step.

There goes Arthur Snugg. He handles life eternal and is eternally dating someone new.

Alex came back up the stairs and took a seat in my spare office chair.

"Uncle A got a good one this time," Alex said, leaning out the doorway and glancing up the staircase toward his uncle's now-closed office door.

"Talking to Ida Stoner again, I guess." I opened my phone and checked to see if I had any missed calls from Russell.

"The woman makes a mean coffee cake." Alex patted his stomach.

"She is a thoughtful lady." I got up and adjusted the cut flower arrangement of sweet pea and Solomon's seal that Ida had brought me last week when she introduced herself.

"Have you checked out her farm yet, Mel?"

"No, Alex, why would I do that?" My brow knotted up in puzzlement.

"J.J. and I did. It's a few miles outside of Pleasantview. Got to make sure Uncle A's dates are on the up and up. Man, the place is laid out."

J.J. appeared around the corner.

"Who's laid out? I didn't dress anybody today." He hurried down the hallway and peered in both the Rose and Lilac rooms before returning to lean against my office door.

J.J. handed Alex an issue of Funeral Home Weekly and then tore open a bag of chocolates and began to read over Alex's shoulder as he popped the candy one by one into his mouth.

"Your uncle said you two have work to do. I know I have a ton." I pulled up the PowerPoint I created last week on my computer to market our pre-planning packages. The title *Bury Me in 24 Easy, Interest-Free Payments* filled the screen. I looked toward Alex, my gaze firmly fixed on him as I attempted to raise my eyebrows like his uncle does when he wants the twins to listen.

"Let's go, J.J., that's our cue to start work. I have those front hedges to trim." Alex stood and grabbed the candy from his twin's hand. He raced out the funeral home doors with J.J. close behind.

The rest of Monday went by quickly with invoicing, insurance claims, and inventory of prayer cards.

Before I knew it, the twins and their uncle were saying goodnight as the paw on my cat wall clock ticked to 4:00. I locked the funeral home and, with my list in hand, hurried to Blue Betty. Today's "Old Friend List" and my time management skills led me to Davis & Held's Pharmacy first, and then, if time permitted, I could drive to Tim's Frosty Delight, owned by Tim McCoy, at the perfect time to treat myself to ice cream. I wanted to meet with Julie

Paine, but I neglected to ask Claire where she was staying.

Davis & Held Pharmacy is located about three miles outside of Pleasantview. I hadn't heard from Russell all day, so I decided I would try to phone him on the drive. He picked up on the fifth ring.

"Hey babe, nothing important, just saying I miss you."

"Those are the best words I've heard all day. I'm sorry I didn't call you today. It's been nuts. Now, we have an accident. I'm en route to it."

"Nobody hurt, I hope." I could hear sirens in the background of our call.

"Doesn't sound like it. Ambulances called out though." Russell's voice turned soft. "How's my girl doing today?"

"Slightly better. I decided to get some air and take a ride tonight. I need to go to the pharmacy to pick up a few things, and I am craving ice cream." I rolled down the window in Blue Betty and stuck my left arm out, feeling the breeze go by as I drove.

"You're not driving around hunting old classmates, are you, Mel?"

"Russell, I know you are always trying to protect me, but she had an appointment with me for some reason," I said, my voice level and easy.

"True, but, as of right now, for all we know, maybe she wanted you to pre-plan her funeral."

"Do you hear yourself? She was 29 years old. I ask you, what 29-year-old pre-plans their funeral? You know…you're right, Russell! She probably made an appointment to commiserate about being the top two or make that the only two on the 'B list!'" I gasped. My voice was getting hysterical. This wasn't my intention when I called him, and we were rehashing our conversation of yesterday again.

"Oh, I'm losing it." I put both hands back on Blue Betty's steering wheel. "I'm sorry! Did any of her health reports list diabetes, high blood pressure, or any terminal ailments? Or did you find out if she had any allergies?"

"No. I'm sorry. I've upset you again. Do you want me to come over after my shift tonight? I will you know."

"No, that's okay." I let out a loud sigh. "I guess witnessing her die is bothering me more than I realized. I'll be okay. I'll text you later when I get home."

"Okay, and please promise me you won't go investigating Stephanie and her death."

"I promise," I said in as sweet a voice as I could.

Technically, I wasn't lying. I wasn't investigating Stephanie and her death; I was visiting the people I thought might know something about why she came to me.

"I just pulled up on the accident. Text me, Mel," Russell said gently.

"I promise," I said again with more enthusiasm than I felt. Tracking down old high school friends this weekend was causing friction between me and Russell, and making me exhausted and emotionally drained. So far, besides the Hoffs acting suspicious, all I have found out is that Lenny Blane could give a great sermon, but does he practice what he preaches?

I stepped down hard on the gas pedal and gunned Blue Betty past Davis & Held's Pharmacy. If ever I needed ice cream, it was now. When I checked earlier, Tim's Frosty Delight was open until 8:00 p.m. I made the executive decision that eating ice cream should always come before buying toothpaste.

Luckily, Tim McCoy's ice cream shop wasn't too far of a drive, and then I could go to Davis & Held's Pharmacy on my way home. When I turned off Route 50, the speed limit in the small town of St. Mare was 25 mph.

Looking around at the brick and siding two-story homes, all with beautifully landscaped yards, I pictured Tim. We had geometry and science lab together. He never raised his hand or shouted out the answer, but when Mr. Simmons or Ms. Clark called on him, he always responded correctly. And he was a wiz with dry ice.

The ice cream shop was located on Rose Street, a picturesque, level road. Double-hung lamp posts and large concrete planters filled with seasonal flowers decorated the sidewalks.

It's a good thing the road is flat. Now that two of my bricks are MIA.

Parking signs informed me that St. Mare ticketed 24 hours a day. Luckily, the ice cream shop had its own newly paved parking lot, so I didn't need to worry about level streets or parking. The front of the A-framed structure was painted with splashes of red, white, and blue. Attached to the side of the building was a large smiling cone. There was an ordering window with a display board above it revealing their flavors for soft ice cream, hard ice cream, and frozen yogurt. A big, neon ice cream sign blinked "Open-We Have Your Flavor." The ice cream flavor of the day–chocolate raspberry swirl.

A tall, athletically built woman around my age with chic, spiked, brunette hair stood at the order window.

"How can I help you?" Her smile spread up to her eyes.

"Hi, can I have a small…wait, make that a medium chocolate raspberry swirl cone."

"Cake or sugar?" she asked as she jotted it down on her tablet.

"Cake, please."

"Okay, that will be $3.89."

I dug into my purse for money and handed it to her.

"Is this ice cream shop owned by Tim McCoy?"

"It sure is. Tim and I own it. I'm his wife, Sarah." She wiped her hands on her apron.

I wanted to shout, "I need ice cream and answers." But instead, I said, "I'm Melody. It's great to meet you. I went to school with Tim and heard he bought an ice cream shop in this area. Is he here?" I looked around the empty parking lot.

"He's in the back. I can get him," she said as she expertly scooped the chocolate raspberry swirl ice cream, piled it on the cone, and handed it to me. "What did you say your name was again?"

"Melody Shore."

Five minutes later, Tim and Sarah appeared from a side door of the shop.

I quickly swallowed my last bite of cone and did my best to wipe my chilled lips, which I was sure were now dyed raspberry and possibly had smears of ice cream still on them. I silently wished Russell were here, remembering our first ice cream date and silly ice cream kisses.

"Hi, I'm Tim," he said. He brushed his hand through his curly brown hair and gave me a boyish grin causing his chin dimple to stretch. He extended his hand. "My wife said we went to college together. I'm sorry, my mind is frozen from too much time in the cooler. Did we take a class together?"

He doesn't remember me?

"Um," I stuttered, "high school, we had geometry together and science lab. I'm Melody, and my best friend is Claire Cottage, and I was Stephanie Gregor's lab partner."

Tim's youthful face froze, and for a fleeting moment, there was glaring eye contact between him and his wife, Sarah. Sarah quickly looked away, and he shuffled his feet.

"I am going back inside." Sarah McCoy turned away and began to walk. "Tim, make the visit with your old friend quick. You have work to do."

She went into her building, not even bothering to say goodbye.

Once Sarah was gone, Tim spoke.

"Melody, of course. You were the reason Stephanie could make it through that class." He ran his hands over his distressed, dark-wash jeans. "I heard about her passing away. Do you know any details? No one seems to know anything."

"No other than speaking to Lenny Blane. I know she needed my help. Do you have any idea why, Tim?"

"Help. With what?" Tim asked.

"That's what I am trying to figure out."

"Lenny informed you of her death?" A confused look crossed Tim's face.

"Yeah. How did you find out Stephanie had passed away? From Rachel and Brandon?"

"So, what brings you out here to see me?" Tim asked.

Avoiding my question.

"We had an appointment to meet, and she passed away before we could talk. I thought you might know what she needed help with. That, and ice cream." I motioned toward his shop. "I thought it might be easier to talk to people now before the wedding."

A puzzled look crossed Tim's face again.

I changed the subject.

"I hear your dad owns the Admiral Hotel. How is your dad doing?"

"Okay, I guess. Yeah, it's been nothing but trouble for me since he bought it." Tim's eyes cast downward. Then, he looked up and over my shoulder towards his store. "I was working here at the store the day Stephanie passed away. I do ice cream inventory on Fridays."

Why is he so specific about what he does on Fridays? After that comment, I'm definitely not telling Tim that I was with Stephanie when she passed away.

"I wasn't asking for your alibi, Tim."

"Right," he said, looking toward the door he had come out of.

As if on cue, his wife came hustling out the side door. She gave us both a flagrant look and then heaved a large garbage bag into the dumpster. She slammed down the top and placed bricks to secure the contents. Right before she smashed down the lid I thought I saw ferns and a mask poking out of the top of the bag. It looked similar to the mask in Stephanie's apartment and at *The Artisan.*

Sarah McCoy stomped back into her shop.

"I have to get back to work. Ice cream doesn't sell itself," Tim stammered before quickly turning and almost running back toward his store. He pulled open the side door, and it closed swiftly with a bang.

Huh? No goodbye from Tim either.

I wanted to ask more questions, but after Tim's comments and Sarah's actions, I didn't think going back up to the order window was going to melt either of them into talking more to me. Tim, Sarah, and their ice cream shop had left a queasy feeling in my stomach.

Perhaps I am too boldly seeking people out. I had no backup. Russell knew I was getting ice cream, but he wouldn't think I would go to St. Mare for a treat. What if Tim and his sweet/not sweet Sarah had hit me over the head, put me in their cooler, and made me into a Popsicle? Been there, done that. One time in a freezer was more than enough for this girl. Perhaps I should head home and rethink this whole tracking down old friends.

I ditched visiting Davis & Held's Pharmacy. Instead, I drove to the heart of Pleasantview and down Main Street.

"Are you at the station?" I asked Russell when he answered his phone.

"Be there in about ten minutes. Everything okay, Mel?"

"Yeah, it will be once I see you. I'm driving by Taco Dave's. Can I bring dinner?" I pulled Blue Betty into Russell's favorite taco restaurant.

"We just had tacos, but I could eat them every night. So, yep, the usual, hard-shelled, and lots of hot sauce," Russell answered.

I stopped for tacos and headed to the police station.

Pleasantview Police Station is a one-story, gray brick building. From the outside, it's not very welcoming. However, the sight of Russell was very welcoming.

"Well, did your ride make you feel better?" Russell asked, holding open the door.

Maybe I am spooking myself about Tim and Sarah McCoy. I'm sure an ice cream store owner has to do inventory. But I'm also sure Sarah McCoy was throwing out a mask very similar to the ones I keep seeing.

"Yep, the fresh air and seeing you are helping." I closed his door, and he gave me a much-needed long kiss. Then, I told him about Tim and Sarah McCoy.

"So, let me get this straight," Russell said, pulling out his notebook and motioning for me to take a seat. "You decided to drive two towns over to get ice cream because the shop is owned by a former classmate, and you asked if he knew why Stephanie had sought you out." Russell's voice was level but guarded.

I nodded.

"Tim McCoy told you he didn't know anything, and he was taking inventory of ice cream when Stephanie passed away."

"Yeah, it's crazy, Russell. I know they know something because I saw them make eye contact when I mentioned Stephanie, and I could swear that right before I left, Tim's wife, Sarah, came out of their shop and threw out garbage, and a mask was sticking from the trash. It was just like one I had seen at Stephanie's apartment, and there is a similar one at *The Artisan*. We saw it Saturday night."

"You are observant, Mel. I don't think the masks have anything to do with Stephanie dying, but it is a strange coincidence." Russell put down his notebook. "You would make a great detective." He wrapped his arms around me, and I melted into him. "And…" Russell lifted my chin so our eyes met. "I know, even though I worry about you, there is nothing I can do to stop you. So, please just be careful."

"I will."

"Now, let's eat these," Russell said, stepping toward his desk and unwrapping the taco bag.

After happily munching tacos, Russell had to go back out, but I stayed to feed and play with a bunch of kittens that he and his second-in-command, Kenneth, had rescued from an abandoned building. Because it was later in the evening, and there was no one at the Furry Friends Animal Shelter to process new pets, they had them in a small holding area at the jail.

The kittens were only about three to four weeks old. One of the litter was a black and white kitten. He reminded me of my tuxedo-marked cat, Shady. He was the runt, and without his mom, I worried he wouldn't survive. The other kittens happily lapped milk from the bowl Kenneth had poured, but it was foreign to the little black and white kitten, whom I named Bernard, calling him Bernie for short. After trying to splash his paws in the milk and getting no response, I decided an eye dropper may be the best way to feed him. Feeling full and reassured again, I told Kenneth I would be back as I was going to run to a pharmacy and get an eye dropper. I knew just the pharmacy I wanted to go to.

Davis & Held's Pharmacy is located on Sundown Drive outside of Pleasantview. I had never been there as I use Doc's in the heart of town on Eighth Street.

On the way, I called to see whether Lindsey worked there and if she was the pharmacist on duty. The man who answered said, "Yes, Lindsey, the owner, is working this evening. Would you like to be connected?" I mumbled no and hung up.

The pharmacy was hard to spot, located between a karate studio and a gyro shop, each broadcasting their store with huge banners. It was small, with one aisle offering card selections and a few aisles of health and beauty items. The prescriptions were filled in a small area sectioned off with a laminated countertop that ran the back width of the store. I browsed the aisles for several moments. There was a man and a woman in the far back area and a gentleman working the counter. It was easy to recognize Lindsey as she hadn't changed much since high school. She still wore her long brunette hair pulled up in a ponytail and dressed as she had in high school, ready to join any exercise class at any moment. Underneath her lab coat, she wore a pair of yoga pants and a T-shirt with the words "Davis & Held Pharmacy" embossed across the chest.

I picked up two eye droppers. One was a plain, easy-to-use dropper, and the other was a premium, high-tech gadget that was calibrated and offered a bent tip. I also took two different teeth whitening products to the counter in case the eye dropper conversation made me look like a drip. The first kit promised to whiten my teeth in an hour or my money back, and the second was a toothpaste with a whitening agent. Even if the conversation didn't draw any leads, I would get an education in teeth whitening products. I decided against picking up my regular toothpaste, vitamins, and contact solution. I would get them at Doc's with my savings card.

Approaching the guy behind the counter, I asked if I could talk to Lindsey. He looked genuinely relieved that I didn't want to ring my purchases up yet. He was having a battle with the register tape that had run out, and the tape was winning.

With the size of the pharmacy, Lindsey couldn't help but overhear me asking for her by name.

She looked up and smiled warmly. Then, recognition hit her face.

"Melody Shore. Wow!" Lindsey took a step backward and gave me a once-over. "I'm sorry. I didn't recognize you at first without your braces. It's been a long time. I heard you moved back to Pleasantview. I'm sorry I haven't made any effort to seek you out and get together."

"About ten years. How have you been?" I asked.

"I'm fine, but what's wrong with you?" Her eyes traveled from my head to my toes and back again. "I mean, what brings you to Davis & Held's today?" she asked, her face painted into a smile.

"Well, I have a couple of questions. Looks like you're not busy." I glanced around the empty pharmacy. "I mean, if you have time?" I stared at her, not blinking, daring her to say no.

When she said nothing, I broke my stare and looked down at my eye dropper selection and teeth whitening products.

I wish I had thought of a better intro than stopping to see someone after 10 years to ask about teeth whitening.

"Guys, we went to school together," she said to her male coworkers. Then, she turned to me. "We are filling late-day orders before we close, but I guess I can talk for a few minutes."

Lindsey pointed toward a "no entrance" door. I followed her through it into an employee lounge. It contained a round table and four chairs. There was a small kitchen set up and a table with a TV that was on and tuned to a reality show.

"Have a seat, Melody."

I pulled out a chair and sat down. Lindsey went to the refrigerator and took out a fruit-infused water bottle.

"What really brings you here?" She swiftly sliced a lime from a bowl on her countertop, dropped it into the bottle, added water, and turned toward me, knife still in hand.

I went with the truth, silently wishing that I had told Kenneth which pharmacy I was going to.

"Lindsey, did you know Stephanie Gregor passed away?"

"I do. Was she sick?" she asked a little too earnestly.

"Actually, I think foul play may have been involved." My voice lowered and sped up when saying the words foul play.

At that point, she put the knife down, took a drink from her lime water, and came and sat at the table.

"Why would you think that?"

"Because I was there."

Russell would have called this a rookie move, but I lost my poise. Once I told her, I began to shake in front of a woman I hadn't seen in ten years.

"Have you seen a doctor for anxiety?" Lindsey quietly asked.

She got up and brought a box of tissues to the table.

"If you have a prescription, I can fill it, but I can't do favors for classmates or old friends." She gave me a tight-lipped smile.

I blew my nose and took a few deep breaths.

"You said you were with Stephanie when she passed away. Why?" she asked, her voice strangely rising as if she demanded an answer.

I didn't want to explain any more to her, so rather than answer, I loudly blew my nose again.

"Are the police investigating?" she asked, her voice softer now.

"I'm sure it's an active investigation," I said, regaining my composure.

"Do you have any idea how she died?" Lindsey asked, her face inches from mine.

"No, but have you and Stephanie stayed friends since we graduated?" I asked.

Lindsey glanced down at her hands. It was hard not to notice that her left ring finger held a large, sparkling, rose gold wedding band set. The ring, her only piece of jewelry, looked out of place on a woman who otherwise appeared plain.

"Not since Dave."

"Dave?"

"Dave, my husband, Dave Davis." She straightened her back and pulled her ponytail tight.

She acted as if I should know who he was, as if everyone knew Dave Davis. I made a mental note to do a little research on her husband when I returned home.

"So you haven't seen her in how many years?" I asked.

Lindsey's neck prickled, and her collarbone and chest turned red. I reached toward my neck and rubbed.

"When did this conversation turn to questioning?" she asked.

"Did you see her last week?" I asked.

"Look, Melody, unless you are the police, and I don't think you are, I don't need to answer. What I do is none of your business. I am done answering questions." She stood. "I have a pharmacy to run." Lindsey motioned for me to get up, also. "But, if you find out about funeral arrangements, I would like to pay my respects," she said, her voice now dripping with false sweetness.

Lindsey has something to hide, but I can't tell if it's personal or related to Stephanie. I wonder if she will bring Dave Davis to any viewing. I better not ask.

"Sorry, I'm still upset over Stephanie. Perhaps she had a heart condition. She didn't look good from the last time I saw her."

I thought I saw a slight smile on the corner of Lindsey's mouth.

"How horrible for you, Melody. Did you two stay friends long distance?"

"I didn't move that far, Lindsey. I lived two hours away."

"Where were you two again when she passed away?" Lindsey came back over to me and sat down, drawing her chair close.

"She came into *The Peaceful Rest Funeral Home,* where I'm employed."

I took a deep breath and waited for her response.

Lindsey was quiet.

"She had an invitation to Rachel and Brandon's wedding," I said, filling the silence.

The register guy poked his head into the room and gestured in the direction of a phone on a stand. "Lindsey, call for you. I transferred it in here."

Lindsey quickly moved to the phone on the other side of the room. I stayed seated.

"I have to take this. One of the guys will help you with your purchases." She covered the phone receiver and said, "Let's get together soon. It's been too long." She motioned toward the door back into the pharmacy, her finger pointing once again in the direction I was to follow.

Lindsey stood silently waiting for me to leave before taking her call. I picked up my eye droppers and teeth whitening products and exited the room. The register guy went back behind the counter, and the other guy stood motionless, his head bent down in a pill-counting ponder. I walked to the dropper aisle and then back to the teeth whitening aisle and reshelved the items. On the way back to the Pleasantview Police Station, I stopped at Doc's and purchased a $1.00 eye dropper for Bernie, my normal toothpaste, vitamins, and contact solution.

When I returned to the police station, Bernie was happy to see me. He appreciated the eye dropper feeding and was soon fast asleep in my lap. I gently laid him next to his siblings and headed home.

Back at my apartment, I redid the "Old Friend List." If someone had harmed Stephanie, these "friends" were on my "suspect" list.

<u>My Top Six "Friends/Suspects"</u>

1. Brandon Hoff and/or Rachel Grey (The engaged couple. If they did anything to Stephanie, they won't be pouring drinks from the prison bar. I can see the headlines now - Newlywed bar owners on tap for murder.)

2.   Tim McCoy and/or Sarah McCoy (The ice cream shop owners who have more to hide than the calories in their ice cream.)

3.   Lindsey Held (What is up with her? I know we haven't seen each other in years, but that sure was a strange conversation. Who is Dave Davis?)

4.   Lenny Blane (I hope I am wrong about him. My mother would never forgive me if I were involved in a minister's arrest.)

<u>Still to talk to</u>

5.   Julie Paine, DC

6.   Jake Evans

Before going to bed, I did some research on Dave Davis. Dave had graduated as a pharmacist from the same university as Lindsey. Upon graduation, he married the daughter of a very wealthy business owner from Ohio. Dave opened a pharmacy in Ohio, and all seemed to be going well for him until Dave's wife caught Dave filling more than his customers' prescription needs. Dave got himself a lawyer, and he and his wife quietly settled out of court for a hefty, undisclosed amount. Shortly thereafter, real estate transactions list Dave as solely owning a one-million-dollar home about 40 minutes from Pleasantview.

It was right after this that social media pictures show him reconnecting with Lindsey, and a short eight months later, he professed his love to her. They united in marriage, and Lindsey's sole proprietorship, Held's Pharmacy, became Davis & Held. While informative, none of this information answered my question of why Lindsey couldn't remain friends with Stephanie after she married Dave Davis.

When I entered my fishbowl office on Tuesday, it was apparent that Arthur Snugg had been in either late last evening or early that morning. Snugg plastered sticky notes on my computer screen and desk, and, in case I didn't see them, he left a tablet on my chair.

The first one on my computer screen said he was taking today off to help Ida Stoner in her garden, and he had scheduled an appointment for 11:00 for me to please handle. The second one on my desk said that the file for the appointment was in his office, and the tablet on my chair said, "Low on decaf. Can you pick that up at the warehouse club? Also, mints for the dishes." In parentheses, he wrote, (I need to join the club.)

I walked up the mahogany staircase, my black Mary Jane shoes squeaking with each step. The file lying in the center of Arthur Snugg's immaculate office desk was titled "Stephanie Gregor."

Don Gregor was my 11:00 appointment. After the autopsy, the coroner would release the body to Old Peaceful. I went to the kitchenette, made a cup of coffee, and then paced the lobby for five minutes before I sat back down and looked through her file.

Darn. It only contains the funeral home forms that Snugg wants filled out for her arrangements.

The phones were relatively calm for a Tuesday and we had no clients in the viewing area. Alex and J.J. were busy with lawn maintenance. I could see their tractors in a heated race crisscrossing across the cemetery lawn, dodging tombstones as they drove.

I had just removed the dead flowers from their vases and was draining the water down the sink when I heard a loud crack, pop, and rumble. I rushed to the window. A bright red Chrysler PT Cruiser pulled into the lot, smoke pouring from its tailpipe.

A small man, only about 5'7" tall, exited the car. He appeared to be in his late 50s, had a receded hairline, and had glasses in the breast pocket of his short-sleeved, collared shirt.

"Hello." The man looked nervously around the funeral home as he adjusted the belt of his pants, pulling it up over his slight paunch.

I exited my office and extended my hand in greeting.

"You must be Mr. Gregor, Stephanie's father. I'm Melody Shore. I'm so sorry for your loss."

Don Gregor's whole body shook as he clutched my hand.

"Do you have some water or something I could have before we begin?"

"Sure. Please, take a seat in my office." I pointed toward my one guest chair. "I will be right back."

In the kitchenette, I filled our best silver pitcher with water and ice cubes, took a glass for him from the cupboard, and returned to my office. I poured Don Gregor his water, set the pitcher on my filing cabinet, and sat down at my desk. After a few sips, his hands quit fidgeting with his collared shirt and belt. I opened Stephanie's file and began with the standard arrangement speech that Arthur Snugg had given me, and I tweaked it to make it less formal.

"First, let me say that we appreciate you choosing us to handle your loved one's arrangements. Please don't feel pressured about anything; we are here to help you."

Snugg had everything labeled by package deals, or you could pick à la carte off the list should you prefer that.

I placed the forms in front of Don Gregor.

"As you can see, we have the 'Ultimate Send Off,' the 'Between Heaven and Earth,' and the 'Simple Life' packages to choose from."

As Don Gregor rocked in my stationary chair, nodding and giving three-word answers, "Okay, that's fine," "Yes, that one," I worked through Snugg's checklist.

"Do you have an outfit you would like her laid out in?"

A blank stare was my answer to this question.

Fifteen minutes later, with the forms mostly filled out and Don Gregor's signature getting a workout, I said, "Mr. Gregor, perhaps it would help put you at ease to drive around to see the beautiful gardens we have and available plots."

"Yes, fresh air would be great," he said, standing and rushing out the funeral home's front door.

As we drove around in Snugg's beige PT Cruiser, he inquired whether I could help him with flowers, as he no longer lived in town. Then, I turned the conversation to Stephanie.

"What did Stephanie do for a living, Mr. Gregor?" I asked.

"She's a decorator."

That confirms what the woman outside Stephanie's duplex said.

"Where did she work?" I stopped the Cruiser, reached into my pocket, got out a mini tablet, and began to jot down notes. Don Gregor eyed me curiously. I put my tablet away.

"She was an independent contractor." He stopped talking and glanced around the PT's interior. "Do you happen to have a tissue?" he asked.

I reached across, pushed open the glove box, and handed him a small tissue box that Snugg keeps stocked in each vehicle. He blew his nose, and I continued.

"Mr. Gregor, did Stephanie have any health problems?"

Don Gregor looked at me wide-eyed.

"I mean, it is none of my business, but she was so young…my age."

"I know. I can't believe it myself. How does someone so young die?" Don Gregor produced a handkerchief from his pant pocket and wiped his forehead.

After picking a plot at the Garden of Peace, he said, "Melody, I'm afraid I don't know any ministers. Can you please assist me in having someone give a blessing service?"

"Sure, I have several I can speak to…in fact, one is a former classmate of Stephanie's. Would you like me to phone him?" I asked.

Don Gregor agreed.

"Did she have a steady boyfriend?"

"I remember that high school guy. I don't know if she has a current boyfriend, though." Don Gregor coughed and choked back a sob. "I guess I will have to get used to saying had."

I parked the funeral home's PT Cruiser, and we got out and stood awkwardly in the parking lot.

"The guy you are referring to, was his name Jake?"

"I think, maybe." His thick brows knotted up. "How would you know?" he asked.

At that point, I decided to tell Don Gregor about knowing Stephanie in school and also how I had tried to save her. I ended it with, "If it's any comfort, she didn't die alone. I was there holding her hand, being a friend."

"That is very comforting to hear." He reached forward and patted my shoulder.

"Mr. Gregor, Stephanie made an appointment last week to see me. Do you know why?"

"No. She phoned me two weeks ago. We haven't spoken in over a month. She asked me to come see her. I said I needed to clear a few things up at work, and I could come this week." He sighed heavily. "I wish I hadn't procrastinated. I would have had a chance to see her one more time."

"Do you know why? I mean, why did she want you to visit?"

"Yes, sort of. When we talked, she seemed excited. Said she had a big contract and had received an advance. She wanted me to hold the money until she worked out the details." Don Gregor stood tall.

"She wanted you to hold her money?" *I wonder if someone got to her and the money first. The one room in her home looked in disarray.*

"Yeah, I guess my little girl had finally grown up." He cleared his throat. "Did she bring any possessions with her when she came in?"

"No. Sorry." *Other than the wedding invite and some groceries.*

"I truly appreciate you telling me that," Don Gregor said as he enveloped me in a hug. "I'm so thankful that Stephanie was with you, Melody, when she passed away."

Then he quickly dropped his hug and clenched his fists. His eyes were wide.

"Wait a minute. I've been trying to place your last name since you told me it. Are you Laverne Shore's daughter?" Don Gregor took a few steps backward.

"Yes, I am, and I know my mom can come off a bit strong."

"That's putting it nicely. Maybe I should rethink using The Peaceful Rest."

"Mr. Gregor, let me assure you I take my job very seriously, and my boss, Arthur Snugg, does also. Stephanie's funeral is in good hands." I folded my hands in front of me and stood still.

Don Gregor looked around the parking lot. After a long minute, he unclenched his fists and spoke.

"I apologize. You can imagine how upset I am. We will continue as planned; just please don't tell your mother I am in town for my daughter's funeral."

"Um, okay."

"She won't be attending, will she?"

"I'm…"

He hurried off to his car, muttering under his breath.

"Goodbye, Mr. Gregor," I said over the roar of his engine.

The flowers, clothing, and minister were now my responsibility. I went back into the funeral home and made another cup of coffee. This time, I added the Baileys that Arthur Snugg keeps on hand for when times get tough. Then, I got to work on Stephanie's funeral.

In the lower level of The Peaceful Rest, we have a closet of clothing that is available for purchase should the deceased's family not provide an outfit for a viewing. I quickly chose a rose-colored dress for her and added it to Don Gregor's bill at cost. Next, I pulled up a list of florists who I thought had provided tasteful, reasonably priced floral arrangements in the past and sat picking Stephanie's flowers. After several phone calls to get the best price, I decided on a spray of pink roses with waxflower and greenery for above the casket and two carnation arrangements that would fit into the vases we have downstairs as accents.

My only task after that was to contact Lenny Blane.

Finding Lenny's phone number by looking up the church was the simple part. Calling and not being able to see his expression when he heard it was me on the phone was the hard part.

I picked up the phone and dialed.

"Faith Church."

"Pastor Blane, please. I'm calling from The Peaceful Rest Funeral Home and Cemetery."

"Certainly. Hold a moment."

Several minutes later, Lenny answered the phone.

"Lenny, it's Melody Shore."

One, two, three seconds went by as I watched the tail of my cat wall clock tick away the time.

"Melody, how can I help you?"

"Lenny, there is an investigation into Stephanie Gregor's death."

Silence. More clock ticking.

"I know, Melody. The police spoke to us yesterday. If you are calling because you need to talk to someone, I could connect you with our grief counselor, Ben."

"Ben? The organist/collection manager/ groundskeeper is a grief counselor, too? Is he single? Claire is. I mean…no, ignore my comments. Speaking to Ben won't be necessary. *At least not right now.* The reason for my call is work-related." I opened my file cabinet, took out my stash of mints, and tore open a wrapper.

"Work-related?"

"Yes, I'm the Arrangement Coordinator at The Peaceful Rest Funeral Home and Cemetery."

My self-appointed title. I really need to talk to Arthur Snugg about allowing me to have business cards printed with that on them.

Lenny was silent, and then he cleared his throat. "I'm not in the market for arrangements."

"Stephanie's father was in today." I popped the mint into my mouth. When Lenny said nothing, I continued, "He has decided to use our cemetery for internment."

"Thank you for letting me know, Melody."

"He's not living in the area anymore and needs our help." I bit the mint and swallowed. "I was hoping, I mean, Don Gregor asked, if you weren't busy tomorrow night, that you could preside over her blessing service?"

A shuffling of papers replaced the silence.

"Tomorrow, Wednesday, yes. Do you have a number for her father so that I can speak to him regarding his wishes?"

After giving Lenny the information for Don Gregor and thanking him, I hung up the phone. I sat eating two more mints and thinking about who he meant when he said, "The police spoke to us."

Maybe he means himself and the other church staff. Did Russell talk to Ben, or does he mean Jake? But why would they talk to the church? Maybe Russell has a lead, and this will all be over soon.

"Hey, Mel," Alex said, coming into the room and dusting grass from his jeans. "It's quitting time. Want to join us over at Mickey's?"

Mickey's is Alex and J.J.'s favorite bar. It is right across the street, and their wings and drink specials can't be beat.

"I could use a drink, but…"

"They got a new dartboard," J.J. said, bounding up the last two steps of the lower-level staircase with a hop. He flexed his arm and mimicked a dart throw, followed by clasping his hands together and giving a rounding cheer. "Rematch, Mel?"

"Thanks, guys. Raincheck for another time. I will keep my title intact."

The twins both gave me frown faces and then hurried out the door in a race toward Mickey's.

As much as their evening sounded like the perfect ending to my day, I knew I needed to concentrate on trying to find out why Stephanie came to see me. I only had one evening until her service and three days until the wedding.

I phoned Claire.

"Melody, everything okay?" Claire asked.

"Yes. I have the funeral arrangements for Stephanie. It will be here at Old Peaceful, a blessing service. Tomorrow, starting at 6:00." I drummed my pen on my desk.

"Oh geez. I'm sorry, Melody. I thought it would be over in Foxmoor."

"I guess because Don Gregor is originally from Pleasantview and he trusts Snugg, we are handling it." I began to straighten my desk contents. "Claire,

I'm just wondering if you know where Julie is staying while she's in town?"

"Oh, she's at the Admiral Hotel. I was going to call you anyway. We were thinking it would be fun to have a fashion show at my store. I mean, I know you are upset about Stephanie, all of us are, but this would be a chance to be together."

"Who was thinking?" I stood and walked toward the funeral home lobby.

"Julie and me. She said I should invite you, Rachel, and Tim's wife, Sarah. A fun girls' night."

"Claire, you want me to come to a fashion show with people who are going to be together for a wedding this Saturday that I'm not invited to?" My voice cracked as I spoke and paced the lobby. Ten steps toward the Rose Room, a quick turn to test the dryness of the large Peace Lily that Stephanie had fallen over, and back toward the Rose Room.

"Yes, I do."

Silence filled the airwaves between my best friend and me.

"Come on, Melody," Claire said, breaking the silence. "I'll be there, and it will be fun. I promise. Look, I'm sure Rachel feels bad that she didn't invite you. Julie let it slip that her mom is still pretty ticked at your mom."

"So I miss out on the fun and am excluded from the group because my mother spilled the wine and wouldn't read some books?" I walked into the Rose Room, pulled a tissue from one of the three boxes on the end tables, and dabbed at my eyes.

"I know, I agree, it's ridiculous. I still can't figure out why I'm invited, but whatever."

"When is the fashion show?" I crinkled the tissue and tossed it in the trash can.

"Oh, good, you are going to come. I promise you will have fun. It's Friday night. Julie suggested we make it sort of like a bachelorette party fashion show. Jules is providing food and drinks. She checked with the others. They are coming. You're my holdout."

"Oh boy. Sounds like a great time."

"It will be Melody. You need to relax. When I told Jules how stressed you've been, she thought this would be just what you needed."

I bet she did. Claire is going to be really upset if Jules had anything to do with Stephanie's death.

"Claire, is Lindsey invited to your fashion show?"

"No. Jules didn't think it would be a good idea."

"Why not? She used to be friends with Rachel and Julie, and you and me."

"I don't know. I guess I should invite her."

"It's always nice to be invited. And, Claire, since when did you let other people call the shots, especially for a party at your shop?"

"Melody, I think you are overreacting. This isn't high school."

"When I saw Lindsey, she said she hasn't seen anyone from the old group in a long time." I walked back to my office and started to make a list of Claire's party invitees on the tablet Arthur Snugg had left on my desk. "Claire, do you know if Lindsey is going to Rachel and Brandon's wedding?"

"I heard she rsvp'd no. Something about other plans."

"Hmm."

"Melody, can you put aside your search for answers about Stephanie and just come and have fun? We can't bring Stephanie back. These women were our old friends."

"Yeah, old friends who might have played a role in Stephanie's death," I muttered under my breath. "I'm sorry, Claire, I think I'll sit this one out." I collapsed into my office chair.

"Melody, you can't stay locked away in that funeral home forever. You have to get out and live."

"I'm not locked away here. Claire, it's my job. Listen, I have to go. I'll talk to you tomorrow."

"Okay, sure. Listen, I'm sorry if I upset you. You know you're my closest friend. Can you at least think about Friday night?"

"I'll think about it."

"I'll tell you what, come, and put your detective hat down for a night and share some laughs and drinks. On your next payday, I'll let you have a private shopping day in my store with an outfit of your choice 75% off."

"Even that aqua print blouse and white midi skirt you have on a mannequin in your window?" I began to doodle a smiling stick figure on the notepad.

"Yep, and guess what, it has a pearl clutch that I didn't put up because that mannequin's arms don't stay on if I hang anything off them. I need to get that fixed. I just have the arms inside the blouse for form, but they aren't attached to the body."

"Sounds like the title for a low budget scary movie. 'The mannequin with no arms.'"

"Ha-ha, you got that right. Oh, Melody, I can't do this without my bestie. Please come. I'll give you a deep discount on a double strand pearl necklace, too."

"Okay, you talked me into it. I'll come. I mean, what can possibly happen? It's just a small party with old friends." I scribbled lines through my smiling stick pic.

After Claire and I hung up, I looked up the number for *The Artisan*.

I need to find answers and follow up on my mask theory.

"The Artisan, hold please."

Several minutes later, a woman got back on the phone.

"Sorry to keep you waiting. Do you need a reservation for this evening?"

"No. I am calling to inquire as to whether you sell the art on your restaurant hallway walls." I looked toward the lobby and Snugg's framed photos of his father and grandfather.

"Yes, we do. Is there a piece you are looking at?"

This is working pretty well. I should have thought of this sooner.

"The mask piece with the succulents at the top."

"Oh, yes, a very interesting piece. Hold on a minute."

I could hear papers rustling as I waited.

"That piece is $400. I can hold it for you if you like, or I can take your credit card over the phone and ship it to you for $50."

"Wow! Um, who is the artist? Do you know?"

"It says here, Ms. Stephanie Gregor. I can package one of her cards for you in case you want other pieces by her. This is the only piece we have in the store, and I doubt you are going to find it anywhere else. Mr. McCoy is very selective in his art choices." She paused and then said, "I mean, it is a very unique piece."

Mr. McCoy? Does Tim's dad or Tim own The Artisan, too? And it's so unique that Sarah McCoy was throwing her $400 mask out. I wonder if Stephanie gave it to her? But why?

"Hello. Do you need to go get your credit card? I can put you on hold. I have to ring up a customer now."

"Oh, not necessary. I will stop in the store. Thanks for your help."

"Sure."

After my call, I locked up the funeral home, got into Blue Betty, and sat in the parking lot. The warm summer sun beat down through the windshield. I dialed my phone again.

"Admiral Hotel," the receptionist said.

"Can you please connect me to Julie Paine's room?"

As I waited, I drummed my fingers on Blue Betty's steering wheel. Ten drums in, Julie got on the line.

"Hello."

"Julie, it's Melody Shore."

"Oh my gosh, Melody. It's great to hear from you. Claire told me everything. I can't believe you were there when Stephanie passed away. How are you doing?"

"Okay, I guess. I was just calling because…"

"I heard about the wedding invite. You can't hold a mother's actions against a daughter."

I blew out a big puff of air. "Do you remember my mom, Julie?"

"Sure. I haven't had tuna noodle since." Julie let out a little snicker.

"Listen, Julie, I was wondering if we could get together before Friday?"

"Sure. I can only imagine how uptight you are. I'm sure Claire told you I'm a chiropractor. The hotel is renting me a space in the spa to perform adjustments. I'm sure I can get you straightened up and back to feeling yourself. Come by in half an hour."

"Um, I was thinking…"

"Come on, Melody. Let me take a crack at you. I can fix all your problems. I'll see you shortly.

Julie hung up.

What just happened? I wanted to talk to her, but I don't need a chiropractor visit.

I straightened my posture. My neck cracked, and my back gave a little twinge.

At least, I don't think I do.

I dialed my phone again.

Russell answered on the first ring.

"Hey, babe. Everything okay?"

"I guess. Yes. Sort of. Don Gregor is in town, and he came into Old Peaceful today. I handled Stephanie's arrangements."

"Geez, Mel, I'm sorry you had to go through that."

"What he told me is why I called you." I rubbed the back of my neck, which felt very tight now, took a deep breath, and told Russell about Stephanie telling her dad she had a new large contract and received an advance.

"Russell, if foul play is involved in Stephanie's death, it could have something to do with money from that contract."

"It could. Did you ask if he knew with whom and for what, and who paid her the advance?"

"No. I…well, I tried. He realized who I am, or I should say who my mom is. Things sort of ended quickly after that. I didn't get to ask him anything else. Maybe I can talk more to him at the funeral."

"I will ask him," Russell said, his voice weary.

"I also called to tell you I am seeing a chiropractor tonight."

"Let me guess, Julie Paine, D.O."

I could hear Russell shuffling papers.

"Claire told me she's staying at the Admiral Hotel. I contacted her, and we are meeting in the spa area."

"How convenient. Listen, Mel, I can't stop you, just please be careful."

"For sure, and my back has been bothering me. Tomorrow, I will be good as new. Yep, right back in alignment." I sat up straight in my seat as if he could see my posture through the phone.

I could hear the scanner in Russell's patrol car buzzing to life.

"Oh, here's my captain calling," Russell said with a loud sigh.

"I know, you have to go."

The phone was silent.

I didn't get a chance to tell him about calling The Artisan.

At the Admiral Hotel, the receptionist's scowl made her look like she needed an adjustment herself.

"Yes."

Is that a question or an answer?

"Today, I'm here to see Julie Paine. She is a guest here at the hotel." I gave the unfriendly woman a polite smile.

"Do you have an appointment?" She looked down at her desk calendar.

I glanced around the empty lobby.

"Actually, no, but we just spoke, and I've pulled out my back." I stretched like I had seen my mother do when she returned from PT. "I was hoping to get an adjustment."

She stared at me for several quiet seconds.

Great, first Lenny Blane, and then the McCoys, and now the hotel receptionist. I'll be three for three in the asked to leave department.

"You're in luck. She had a cancellation. Fill out these forms, and I will need your insurance card when you are ready."

Huh? Since when does a hotel receptionist handle appointments and insurance claims for hotel guests?

"I don't want to put it through my insurance. I am here for a consult only. We're old friends."

She picked up a mania folder from her desk and thrust it at me. I ruffled through it. The paperwork was as thick as my mother's gossip magazines.

"Fill those out if you want to see the chiropractor." She returned to her magazine reading.

I found a chair, sat, and opened the folder.

First question: Describe where the pain is.

There were two pictures - one depicting the front of a person and one depicting the back. I decided to x the mid-back area.

The rest of the papers concerned my health history, previous chiropractic visits, liability waivers, testaments from patients, and coupons and advertisements for everything from vitamins to TENS machines. I checked a couple of boxes, signed my name, and initialed twelve times before I was finished.

When I approached the plank-top desk again, the receptionist was on the phone. The conversation sounded personal and heated. The phone call seemed to involve a broken hot water tank and a plumber who wanted payment by cash only.

Noticing me listening in, she covered the phone with her one hand and through gritted teeth said, "Down the hall, door on the left."

The only door on the left had a piece of computer paper taped to it. Penciled on the paper were the words "Temporary Spa." The approximately ten-by-ten room was empty. It was painted a soft apricot color. A wooden chair rail circled the room, and several chairs were pushed up to the rail. On a singular end table sat brochures, photos of Julie, and a framed certificate of her degree.

I picked up one of the brochures and just as I flipped it open Julie bounced into the room in a pink, skin-tight leotard and pink and taupe leggings. She wore slipper-type, light tan shoes.

"Melody, no need to use the coupon on there. I'll give you the old friend treatment." She pulled the brochure from my hand and placed it back on the table.

"The receptionist insisted I take these forms."

"That Diane. She's something else. So sweet and funny."

"Oh, she's something."

"Anyway, it's great to see you," Julie said as she glanced over the paperwork I handed her. She put the packet down and gave me a quick hug. "What kind of problem are you having?"

In high school, Julie had shoulder-length, dishwater blond hair and was skinny. Today, she had silky, highlighted, long blond hair. Her skinny build now displayed curves in all the right places. I made a mental note that whether she was involved in Stephanie's death or not, she wouldn't be getting any referrals from me for Russell. If he had a back problem or anything else that needed to be adjusted, I would find an elderly chiropractor for him.

"Julie, you're the one who suggested we meet here. I was hoping to talk to you about Stephanie." I stood up tall and squared my shoulders.

"I did. I guess it's where I am most comfortable. I'm sorry, Melody. Would you like something to drink?" She opened a small refrigerator, pulled out a Vitamin water, and handed it to me. "That will be $4.00. You can pay Diane. I'll give you an adjustment while we talk. Have a seat over here."

She pointed at what looked like a portable massage chair on wheels.

"I travel with it. You never know when you might need it. Now I insist, sit and relax. This will only take a few minutes."

Russell knows I am here.

"My police officer boyfriend is fantastic at massages. He's out in the parking lot waiting. I should tell him to come in, you know, to compare notes." I reached into my bag for my phone.

I doubt she will massage me into pain after that comment.

Julie said nothing. She patted the chair.

I kept the phone in my hand and sat down in her massage chair. After several uncomfortable moments where she lightly massaged my back and I giggled because I am a ticklish person, she moved to sit across from me.

"Melody, Claire told me you work at a funeral home. Is that like a side job?"

"No. I work full-time at a funeral home." I raised my upper body back into an upright sitting position.

"You're not doing any heavy lifting there, are you?" Her expression turned to a look of morbid curiosity.

"No, I handle the day-to-day office needs." I stood.

She gave a half-smile and compressed her lips. "Hmm," she muttered. "Your problem is musculature. Try Ibuprofen. It should help." Julie stood, stretched her back, and said, "If not, don't wait to see a chiropractor." She took a few steps toward the exit door.

"Wait, I want to talk to you about Stephanie."

"It's so sad." Julie's eyes misted over.

"I know. I can't believe it. We were supposed to grow old and then find out when we are in our late

80s that old friends had passed away. Not like this," I said.

"Has your boyfriend found anything out about her death?" Julie asked as she came back toward me and straddled the massage chair. Her hands began massaging the headrest.

"I'm not privy to his investigation."

"Why would there be an investigation?" Julie's eyes grew wide.

"They have to check everything out because of her age."

"Oh. Claire said you were the last to see her, and they don't suspect foul play."

"Well, certainly not foul play by me. We don't know yet what caused her death, though."

I need to talk to Claire. She isn't thinking things through by telling Julie the details. She might be putting me in danger and hampering Russell's investigation with talk like that.

"Julie, were you still close with Stephanie?"

"We used to talk."

"Do you know why she made an appointment instead of just stopping by to see me at the funeral home?"

"Maybe she was being polite, not just dropping in and expecting an old friend favor." Julie's eyes narrowed as her hands clenched down on the headrest cushion.

Huh? You insisted I come here.

"Did you go to her party last Thursday?"

"What party? Why are you questioning me, Melody? You certainly don't think I had anything to do with Stephanie passing away."

"No. Of course not. I was just wondering." *Since it seems Claire is telling her everything.* "Can you believe Rachel didn't invite Stephanie to her wedding?"

"Melody, it sure seems like you are trying to interrogate me. I invited you here to help you out. Claire said you were still a lot of fun, so I invited you to our get-together."

"First of all Julie, it is at Claire's shop. It is Claire who does the…"

"Calm down, Melody."

"You're the one who is getting upset, not me."

"I'm just saying, you are very tight, and if I were you, I would relax. It isn't healthy for you. It can only lead to trouble if you stress and poke your nose around. You might end up finding yourself needing more than an adjustment." Julie looked at her watch and then quickly said, "Just come on Friday. It will be a great time."

She breezed out of the "Temporary Spa" without a backward glance.

On the way home, I drove by Claire's Cottage. It was closed. I tried to call her, but she didn't pick up. When I pulled into my driveway a man sat on the fourth step of the wooden steps that lead to my apartment. His elbows were propped up on his knees, and his hands supported his head. He stared blankly at me. Morgan from the Admiral Hotel was the last person I expected to find waiting for me to come home.

"Morgan, what are you doing here?" I rushed up the steps toward him.

"I guess I should have called…, but neither you nor Claire left a number. And you were the only one to give your full name." He started to get up but swayed. I guided him up the steps, steadied him against the railing, and turned to open my apartment door.

"My lock! It's busted!"

I spun around to face Morgan.

"It wasn't me, Melody." Morgan raised his arms in the air, pursed his lips, and shut his eyes. "I swear," he said.

I pushed my door open and called for Shady. He came out of my bedroom, yawned, hopped onto the couch, and lay back down. I stepped into my apartment and glanced around. I'm not a clean freak, but I could tell things had been moved around and sorted through. I edged toward the open doorway. Gauging Morgan's stance with his hands now on top of his head and his rolling eyes, he would not put up much of a fight if I tried to bolt by him down the steps to safety.

"How did you find my address?"

"I searched the internet, and your name came up twice in Pleasantview. One address was a funeral home…and this one," he said slowly.

"Were you in my apartment before I came home?" I pulled my cell phone from my purse.

"Melody, I would never." He sluggishly walked into my apartment, toward me.

"Someone was!" I shouted, motioning around the room.

"Please calm down." Morgan took a careful step backward, put his hands up to his face, and covered his eyes again. "Let me explain."

"I'm making the call." I waved my cell phone at Morgan, even though he wasn't looking at me, and started to dial Russell's number.

Morgan trudged across the room and collapsed down onto my couch.

"Are you calling an ambulance for me?" he asked, his voice muffled by the throw pillow he fell into. When I didn't answer, he sat halfway up, touched the back of his head, winced, and said, "Maybe ice until help arrives?"

I put my phone down, took a bag of frozen spinach out of my freezer, and handed it to him. He looked at me and then down at the bag.

"For your head, the cold will help with swelling."

My frozen cookie dough probably would work better, but I want to make cookies this weekend and don't want to thaw it too soon.

"What happened to you, Morgan?" I sat down next to him.

"I was parking my truck," Morgan said as he adjusted the spinach bag on his head, "and I saw someone running from your driveway, down the street. When I came up the steps to your apartment, your door lock was busted. I thought something might be fishy so I turned and ran back down the wooden steps to follow them, but my foot must have caught on a step, and I fell backward. I banged my back also." He pulled up his shirt to show me a red welt down his muscular side. "I guess my head hit off the side rail." He lightly touched his head again and groaned.

"I don't think you need an ambulance or stitches." I gently took the spinach bag away from Morgan's hand and examined his head. He had a small red lump forming, jutting out from a matted-down spot on his perfect "Ivy League" haircut.

"Did you get a look at them?" I asked, handing him back the spinach.

"Tall, dressed in a light blue hoody and sweatpants. I couldn't see his face." He managed a smile at me. "Sorry, Melody, just the back of him. Now that I think about it, it's odd as the weather isn't sweatshirt weather."

While Morgan sat holding the spinach, looking like a sad puppy, I walked around my apartment. I keep $50 in a kitchen cupboard and that was still there. Although things had been rummaged through, I couldn't find anything missing. The notebook I had been keeping with my notes regarding old friends was safely in my work bag.

My heart rate slowed, but my mind sped up with worry.

What had they broken in for? Would they come back? I need to call Russell. Would he be mad because I had continued questioning my old friends? Maybe I should try Claire again.

When the spinach turned to peas, Morgan said he felt well enough to drive. He thanked me for allowing him in and said he would see me and Claire at the wedding. Whatever he had come to ask me, he had forgotten or decided not to. Apparently, Morgan had picked up a vibe (or more likely a headache). Being around me was living dangerously.

Once Morgan left, I quickly shut my apartment door and placed a wedge doorstop underneath. I took one of my three kitchen chairs and angled the top of the chair under the door handle. Next, I tied two of my leather rope belts to the handle and then secured one to my fridge and one to my pastry cabinet. No one uninvited was coming in now. Shady, ever inquisitive, walked over and inspected my work. Lastly, I dialed Skip's Hardware on Fifth Street.

"Hey, Skip, it's Melody Shore."

"Hey, your boyfriend just called. Do you want to add to his list?" Skip was a grandfatherly type of man with a hearty laugh and a kind word for each of his customers.

"No, but is Russell coming to the store today to see you?"

"Yes, he will be in shortly. What can I do for you?" Skip began to hum.

"He can save me a trip, maybe." I sat down on my couch and slipped out of my Mary Janes. "Can you tell him my apartment was…" I stopped. I didn't want Skip to know and tell Russell before I spoke to him. Or call my mother. "Um, please tell him I broke my door lock and have him pick me up a new one. Can you key it for me?"

Skip said he would, and after asking me how Arthur Snugg, Alex, and J.J. were doing, we hung up.

Next, I phoned Claire.

"Claire, we need to talk."

"I heard about you and Julie. She phoned me and went on and on. I'm really sorry, Melody. I forgot how Julie could be. I should never have said anything you told me. These past couple of days have been rough on you. I should have been a better friend. Mums the word from now on." Claire's voice was soft and reassuring.

"Thanks, Claire. It's important we don't hamper Russell's investigation." *Or mine.* "I called to tell you someone broke in here, and Morgan was on my steps when I found my apartment door busted."

"What? Are you hurt?"

"No. I'm good. I got home after the break-in." I walked over and checked the belts securing my door. With everything tied securely, I couldn't access my frig until Russell came with a new lock. My stomach growled in disapproval.

"This is getting crazier. The cute coordinator, Morgan, from The Admiral? Boy, I can pick them, can't I?" Claire sighed.

"I don't think he busted in, Claire. He was banged up from trying to catch the guy that did." I sat down on my couch and put my feet up.

"Oh. Is he in the hospital?"

"No. I gave him an ice pack for his bruises, and then he left. I have myself locked in and am waiting for Russell."

"Good. Did he find out anything yet? Any results?"

"None that I know, but if he wasn't suspicious before about Stephanie's death, he will be now. I have a feeling he will be at the funeral home tomorrow night." I got up again, took off the belt secured to the refrigerator, and reached in and grabbed a soda.

"Oh, good, Russell will be with you. In that case, I'll handle checking on Morgan. It will mean I will be skipping the service for Stephanie, though. Are you okay with that? I don't know her family and all that."

"It's okay, Claire. I know it freaks you out to go to funerals, and it will be especially hard tomorrow night, being that it's someone the same age and a former friend. You check on Morgan. I will be fine." I swallowed hard. *At least, I hope so.*

Forty minutes later, I heard a soft knocking.

"Mel, open up. It's me." Russell rattled the broken lock.

I removed the door jamb, chair, and the remaining belt that secured my door. Russell stepped into the room.

"Someone broke in." Russell's voice was a soft growl as he looked at the apparatus I had to secure my door.

"They didn't take anything, at least I don't think so. Not that I have anything worth taking. Aside from my photos of the bridges of Pittsburgh, which my dad and I took, there aren't many items worth stealing." I sat down at my computer. "You know what this proves? There had to be foul play in Stephanie's death. Someone is getting worried that we are on to them. Stephanie had no other health problems that we know of. She had to have been poisoned. Probably over the money she got. Tell me everything the police know."

Russell sighed, shook his head, and reached for me.

I stood and let him envelop me in his outstretched, muscular arms.

"I wish I had the manpower to put a guard on you. Tomorrow night is the funeral service. Until then, please don't go chasing down any more old friends." He kissed the top of my head and tilted my chin up to face his determined eyes. "I couldn't imagine what I would do if someone hurt you."

"Yeah, that person better not mess with me," I said, squeezing him tight.

Stephanie's body arrived Wednesday morning before I did. At exactly 11:11, the elevator opened and Alex and J.J. together pushed Stephanie's pink casket into the Rose Room. The Rose Room is the largest and most prestigious of our two viewing rooms with crystal floor lamps, large wing-back chairs, and dark cherry wood coffee tables.

"Hey Mel, do you want to give some input on your friend's layout?" J.J. asked.

"If you don't mind, can you guys handle it?"

I have to come to terms with what happened last Friday. Stephanie came here for a reason. I have to find answers.

Arthur Snugg and his nephews came down the mahogany staircase from his office at 12:40. Snugg had his suit coat and briefcase in hand. The twins had sport coats on over their t-shirts and khakis.

"Melody, is everything ready for this evening?" He set his briefcase and suit coat down and adjusted his blue and green striped, tiny alligator-decorated tie.

"Yes, Mr. Snugg, the flowers have arrived, and Lenny, I mean Pastor Blane, called to confirm. Oh, and Alex put out the guest book and prayer cards, and he made coffee. J.J. filled the tissues and mints up."

"Thank you, Melody. I know this is a tough one for you." Snugg put his hand on Alex's shoulder.

"Yeah, Mr. Snugg, about that..."

"Are you coming this evening?" Snugg asked with a hopeful look on his face. "I've asked the boys to assist me because I thought you might be tied up with old friends."

"Tied up! Let's hope not!... I mean, I'm planning on it."

"Wonderful, we will see you this evening then." Arthur Snugg nodded to his nephews. The twins filed out the front door.

When Snugg walked toward the door instead of the stairs to his office or the basement, I blurted out, "Wait! Where are you all going?"

"Oh, I neglected to mention, we are headed to one of those pop-up mortician meet and greets this afternoon. We'll be back in plenty of time. It is a good chance to network with potential customers." Arthur Snugg picked up his briefcase and hurried out the door.

I was alone again in the Peaceful Rest with Stephanie.

To pass the time, I started to reorganize my bottom desk drawer. The file I created, titled "Peaceful Rest's Greatest Obits," caught my eye. I pulled it out and began to read some of the interesting obituaries that people had requested we post.

For those who wonder, is there life after death? I'll let you know.

When I said roast me, I meant at a banquet, not by cremation.

Please post the attached seating chart for my service, and distribute handouts/sing-along (probably need about 50 copies if all my buddies and exes come).

Assigned Seating for the service of Doug Peabody
First row: My parrot, Barney; Bubbles, my prize-winning goldfish; my current wife; and Beauty, my king snake. (For Beauty's safety, don't let Beauty and Barney sit next to each other.)

Second row: Bar buddies
Third row: Casino buddies
Fourth row: my ex's, current
girlfriends, and my attorney

Handout-
(Sung to the tune of Row, Row, Row Your
Boat)
  Craps, poker, and drinking beer.
  Every day of the week
  Partying, Partying, Partying,
  Partying
  Peabody's life was sure a dream.

Repeat several times until you get the
room charged up.

No sooner had I put away the funny obits, leaned back in my chair, and closed my eyes when the front door of the funeral home creaked open, and in crept Lindsey Held.

"Melody, it's me, Lindsey. Is it safe to come in?" She hollered loudly as she stood one hand on the door and the other over her eyes.

Apprehensive after our last meeting, I grabbed my pink umbrella for protection and exited my office.

"Lindsey, of course it's safe. Come in. What can I do for you?" I readied my umbrella like a baseball bat.

Lindsey looked nervously around the funeral home lobby and then at me, standing feet planted wide, both hands firmly grasping my umbrella.

"This wasn't a good idea. I better go. You seem busy," she said.

"No. Stay and let's talk. Why are you here?" I set the umbrella down next to one of the high wing-back chairs, but still within quick reach.

"I came to apologize. Right before you came to my store the other day, Dave and I fought. I took my anger out on you. We haven't seen each other in years, and I treated you harshly." Lindsey collapsed into one of the chairs and buried her hands in her face.

"Lindsey, you don't have to apologize to me, but I appreciate it. I came to you looking for answers."

"I don't see how I can help, but I'll try."

"Maybe if you're truthful with me and tell me when you last saw Stephanie and what you talked about, it will help." I moved closer but stayed standing.

"Okay. If you think it will help. I saw her last Thursday night. She invited me and Rachel to her house."

"What for?"

"She wanted to talk to Rachel about her upcoming wedding." Lindsey stood and leaned left and right, her eyes scanning toward the Rose Room and Lilac Room. "Is she here?"

"Stephanie? Yes, Stephanie's here. Do you want to pay your respects?"

Lindsey's eyes widened. She jumped up. "Where?"

"Lindsey, this is a funeral home, and her service is tonight. She is laid out in our Rose Room. I can take you in there if you want." I started toward the Rose Room.

"No. That's okay. I mean, I'll come tonight with Dave."

"Okay. So go on. Why did Stephanie invite you both over? Did you all still get together a lot?"

"No. At least I don't." Lindsey looked down at her wedding ring.

"Why were you there then?" I gently guided her back into a chair and sat next to her.

"She was trying to get me to give her business. Decorate for me. I'm a pharmacist. I told her. What kind of decorations would I need? I mean, if she sold soaps or small crafts or household ornaments, maybe."

"$400 face sculptures with ferns," I said under my breath. "I guess Brandon and Tim are still close?"

"Oh yeah. When Tim's dad bought the Admiral, Brandon talked to Tim, and he set up the wedding plans."

"So Stephanie invited you both over to discuss her decorating and the wedding?"

"She didn't want to talk about the wedding. She was bragging. Told us how she was getting big money to redo the Admiral. She wanted to let Rachel know the contractors were going to start demolishing and rebuilding on Monday."

"So Rachel's wedding theme went from 'anchor's away' to 'under construction'?" I let out an inappropriate chuckle at my humor.

"You always were funny, Melody."

"How did Rachel take it? The hotel being torn apart right before the wedding." I looked toward my office and silently wished I were within reach of a notepad, pen, and phone. The only things near me were a box of tissues and a dish of mints.

"She was fuming mad, said she would tell Brandon, and he would tell Tim to cancel the contract. Stephanie got upset at that. They were really arguing."

"But why would Tim give Stephanie the contract to redo the hotel when he had a wedding scheduled? It's almost like he chose her over Brandon."

"I don't know, but you know Stephanie. Not much has changed with her." Lindsey picked at her fingernails.

"But Tim's married."

"That never stopped her before." Lindsey bit down on her index fingernail.

That sort of makes sense. But why was she coming to see me? She made the appointment with me the week before she knew Rachel would be so upset. Was Rachel mad enough to hurt Stephanie or render her unable to remodel? Or Brandon? Rachel and Brandon remain at the top of my list, that's for sure.

"Melody, I've been straight with you. Now, you need to tell me what you know." Lindsey touched my arm.

"I'm sorry, Lindsey. I appreciate what you told me, but I don't know anything. Even though I date a police officer, any investigation is confidential."

"Oh, sure, I guess I understand. Listen, I better go now. I've got to get back to the pharmacy. Dave will wonder where I am." Lindsey stood and hurried to the door.

I ran after her and grabbed her arm. "Wait, Lindsey. Don't run off."

"I have to go, Melody." She pulled open the door.

"One more question. You told me you haven't been around Stephanie since you married Dave. Why is that?"

"You know Stephanie." Lindsey looked down again at her wedding ring.

"No. Not in years."

"Well, like I told you, the old Stephanie hasn't changed. She is still the flirt."

"She's not still with Jake?"

"I think she goes where there's opportunity. I heard she shows up at Hoff's Bar & Grill all put together, and Rachel is exhausted from cooking and tending her bar. Stephanie plays darts and flirts with Brandon and Tim."

"What about Jake? Do you know where he is living now?"

"No, I don't. Listen, Melody, I have to go. I will see you tonight. Okay."

"Yes, of course."

Lindsey darted out the door. I walked into the Rose Room and looked down at Stephanie. She looked at peace.

Brandon and Tim? No wonder Rachel was upset, and no wonder the change in demeanor for

Sarah McCoy when I mentioned you. Was Sarah's husband, Tim, leaving her home, out of the loop, demoting her from lover to ice cream scoop? Were you the queen of darts?

Back at my apartment, I was relieved to find my door still bolted shut. Once inside and locked in, I fed Shady and gave him extra pets. Then, I ate a small dish of Mom's tuna noodle casserole and washed it down with a diet soda. Next, I dressed for Stephanie's viewing.

I decided on a short, flared, black skirt, tan blouse, and a tan pump shoe with a small heel. Looking in the mirror, I felt my outfit was respecting Stephanie's passing and saying to Jake, "Look at what you missed out on all those years ago in high school when you dated Stephanie instead of asking me out." But, most importantly, the shoes were comfortable and easy to run in should I need to make a quick exit from tonight's viewing.

When I arrived at the funeral home, it was 5:45. All the lights were on, and Alex was standing outside the door as the greeter/doorman. He was dressed in a dark blue suit with a light blue shirt and dark blue tie. As soon as I stepped onto the porch, he looked around and, seeing no one else in sight, he pulled out a comb and attempted to tame down his mop of black hair that fell over his eyes. Then, he let out a low whistle. I walked by him through the door into the funeral home, but not before elbowing him in the stomach.

"Ouch, you shouldn't hurt a guy for looking."

"Russell, no, you, definitely yes," I answered.

Alex hollered after me as I walked across the lobby's red carpet. "Mel, there are only two people so far, a minister and some other guy."

I hurried toward the Rose Room where Stephanie lay.

Lenny and the other man were kneeling in front of the casket. I hung back in the doorway to give them privacy.

I couldn't help but notice that the man kneeling next to Lenny had an ankle monitor on. Had he been standing, I probably wouldn't have noticed it. In the kneeling position, the monitor was easy to see. I walked slowly into the room.

After several minutes, Lenny stood. He put his hand on the shoulder of the other man and bent slightly, speaking so quietly that even though I was now standing directly behind them, bending down slightly myself, I couldn't make out what he was saying.

The man turned his head sideward, and I saw his profile.

"Jake," I whispered, taking a few steps backward.

His hair was no longer blond and wavy. It was cut short, and the hair that used to fall over his beautiful blue eyes, making him look so sexy, had now receded from his forehead.

Lenny put his hand under Jake's armpit and hoisted him to his feet. In Jake's right hand, he held a cane. He turned and limped toward me, using the cane to steady himself. Recognition and a small smile showed on his face.

"Melody, it's nice to see you." Jake stopped, moved his cane to his left hand, and awkwardly extended his heavily tattooed right arm to shake my hand.

"Jake, you too. I'm so sorry about Stephanie." Both of us turned to look at Stephanie lying in her casket.

"Thank you. I don't know what I will do without her."

"You'll get through this and be fine," Lenny said, putting his hand on Jake's shoulder.

Jake smiled slightly, but I could tell he didn't think he would be fine. His calloused hands shook. From his desolate expression and attire of a wrinkled short-sleeve shirt and cargo pants, he was not the man I envisioned he had become. I had always envisioned an executive speaking to a boardroom, dressed in a tailored suit.

At that point, people slowly came into the Rose Room. Our private, three-person conversation was cut short. Stephanie's father, Don Gregor, had yet to arrive, but I noticed Russell was now standing quietly in the hallway. He gave me a slight head nod.

Russell must think someone attending tonight had something to do with Stephanie's sudden passing, otherwise, he wouldn't be here gathering intel and protecting me. I need to tell him what

Lindsey told me, but first, I need to do a little investigating myself.

Most people entering the room went up to Lenny and not to Jake. Jake moved quietly away from the church-related conversations going on around him. He took a seat in one of our wing-backed chairs across the room from Stephanie's casket. I sat down next to him.

Jake looked up momentarily at me and then back down at his shaking, clasped-together hands.

Stephanie's father, Don Gregor, entered the room with two women who resembled Stephanie. They all went as a group to the casket.

Walking behind them was my mother. She was dressed all in black and carried a black clutch and a foil pan. The smell of tuna drifted across the room as she opened the lid. My mother tapped Don Gregor on the back and thrust the unlidded tuna casserole at him. She looked over at me and Jake. She nodded her head and began to speak rapidly to Don Gregor. I couldn't hear what she was saying and didn't want to imagine. Don Gregor and his family mumbled a few words and quickly retreated away from my mom to the hallway. Together, they stood outside the door, sadly munching on Arthur Snugg's mint supply and dabbing their eyes with tissues.

The neighbor of Stephanie with gray and purple-highlighted hair entered the room. She wore purple slacks and a purple and pink blouse. Up at the casket, she and my mother struck up a conversation. I could see them both scowling, whispering, and conspicuously peering around the room at the other attendees.

Instant friends. I knew it.

There were several groups of mourners congregated together in the Rose Room. Tim and Sarah McCoy stood by Lindsey Held, who was clenching onto the arm of a tall man with dark hair and dark eyes. I could tell from the photos I saw online that he was none other than Dave Davis, the pharmacist who liked to make home deliveries. They were joined by Lenny Blane. Conspicuously missing were the future bride and groom, Rachel Grey and Brandon Hoff, and Julie Paine.

"Jake, I can't imagine what you are going through," I said quietly. "You and Stephanie have stayed friends all these years?"

"She was the love of my life."

"Jake, do you know how she died?"

He looked up from his hands and straight at me. His blue eyes pierced into mine. The moment I had wished for ten years ago was coming true. Now, instead of wanting to kiss him, the atmosphere and the circumstances made me want to hug this broken man.

"Do you?" he asked, his blue eyes hopeful.

"Jake, is it possible someone poisoned her?"

"Who would do that?" he asked.

From the look on his face, I couldn't tell whether he was questioning or his mind was reliving something. He glanced around the room.

Everyone else but her family seemed to be having a good time, as loud bursts of laughter erupted several times from the attendees.

Not your customary crowd of mourners. If the person or persons who had committed foul play were in the room, he or she didn't seem to be worried.

"Jake, do you have any idea why she would have come to see me before she passed away?"

He ignored my question.

"She looked so pretty." He stared regretfully at the floor. "The last time I saw her was at the bar."

"What bar?"

"Brandon and Rachel's bar," he said through gritted teeth. "I'm not speaking to them anymore. They're mad at me."

"Brandon and Rachel are mad at you? Why?"

"I guess it's pretty clear, I haven't achieved much since high school. I'm trying to turn my life around with Lenny, um, Pastor Blane's help. But it's a hard road. And now I don't have Stephanie." His speech faded to a whisper on the last sentence.

"Jake, that doesn't explain why Brandon would be angry with you."

"I frequented their bar and sort of ran up a big tab. We were old friends. You know." He turned to me and looked into my questioning eyes.

When I didn't say anything, he looked over at the group of alumni and their significant others who had formed a circle and were laughing and acting like they were anywhere but at a funeral for one of their friends. Jake grimaced and looked back down again at the ground.

"I'm sorry, Jake. Tell me what happened that day you saw Stephanie."

"The whole thing is foggy." He shut his eyes and shook his head from side to side.

I took his shaking hands in mine. "Jake, you can talk to me."

"I cashed my check and drank too much vodka and can't remember much more than Stephanie, Brandon, Tim, and me having a drink with lunch. Well, they had one, I had a few." He put his head in his hands. His whole body began to shake.

"Do you remember what Stephanie was drinking?"

Jake raised his head and looked toward Stephanie's casket.

"Uh, yeah, her favorite. She ordered them a lot. Called a pink lady, maybe. Why?"

"Just wondering. Jake, any information you can give me might help me figure out what happened to Stephanie. Do you remember what you all had to eat?"

"Um, I don't know. I had a burger. I think Rachel's a good cook."

"What did Stephanie have? Try to remember."

He thought for a few moments and said, "Yes." He slapped his knees and continued, "I remember because Tim was teasing about her salad, which had flowers in it. Stephanie thought it was funny. She picked a flower out and put it in her hair. I thought Rachel was going to explode. She said, 'I know you guys think this is just a bar, but it's Brandon's and soon mine. When you criticize my menu items, you criticize me.'" He sighed. "I will never understand women."

"What happened then, Jake?"

"Well, Rachel and Stephanie were fighting like in high school. Stephanie bummed a cigarette from Brandon and went outside. I tried to follow, but before I could get outside, Lenny and Tim's wife showed up."

"Together?"

"Yeah. No. I don't know. Lenny pulled me aside into a booth and really gave it to me." Jake looked over to where Lenny was in conversation with Lindsey and looked quickly back down. He fidgeted in his chair.

"What did he say?"

"He called me a drunk." He looked sadly over at Lenny again. "I guess I am," he muttered humbly.

"Jake, what happened next? What were Brandon and Rachel, Tim and Sarah doing?"

"Sounded like arguing. Marriage stuff. I stayed out of it because Stephanie came back in and pulled me out of the booth. Then, we started to play darts."

"Did you leave together afterward?"

"No. After one game and another drink, she said her head was spinning. She wasn't feeling well. She picked up her purse and left. Lenny told me not to go after her, that I needed to sober up, and that he had had it with me. But I did. I ran after her. She was gone. It was the last time I saw her. I guess I tripped on something outside." He pointed to the cane and bent slightly to rub his monitor-free ankle. "I got arrested for public intoxication outside the bar. I think one of them called the police on me, as they were right there." A tear ran down Jake's cheek.

"Jake, do you remember what day that was? Or what time?"

"I got my check last Friday. I got arrested the same day. I spent Friday after the bar in jail until Lenny bailed me out on Saturday afternoon. This alcohol monitor is part of my terms." Jake lifted his leg slightly and kicked the back of the chair.

Last Friday? The day Stephanie died...

"Jake, what time was this?"

"I don't know, sometime around 12:00 or 1:00, I guess. They have entrusted me to Lenny until my next hearing." He rubbed his hands on his thighs, gripped his knees, and shook his head from side to side. "I need to turn my life around."

So Stephanie wasn't feeling good at the bar on the day she died. And, Mr. Ice Cream Doesn't Sell Itself, Tim McCoy, doesn't have an all-day, iron-clad, ice cream inventory alibi. Also, what was Lenny, a minister, doing at a bar? I thought he went salsa dancing on Fridays. Now, my head was spinning.

We sat for several minutes, neither one of us saying anything, and then I patted his arm. Jake stared straight ahead. His eyes were misted over and tinted red.

I left Jake to his thoughts and headed towards Don Gregor, who was still in the hallway but now speaking to Russell. I made several hand motions pointing toward my office and mouthed, "We need to talk." He quietly nodded. Don Gregor waved at me and started into the room.

I made it halfway across the Rose Room when Lindsey rushed over to me, followed by Lenny.

"Lenny, can you believe Melody was here? I mean, right here." She stomped her foot. "She works here. Can you believe it? It's ironic and creepy." Lindsey hugged herself.

"Lindsey, I'm sure Lenny, being a pastor now, doesn't find a funeral home creepy." I looked toward Lenny for support. He said nothing. "Perhaps Pastor Blane would be interested in putting his church information at your pharmacy. People are always looking for a good church. Lenny, I mean Pastor Blane, gives a great sermon on Sunday nights. Lindsey, you should get his information." I tried to take a few steps toward the lobby, my office, and the only man I trusted in the room, Russell.

My attempt to reach Russell was stopped by an elderly couple who wanted information about the florist that the funeral home feels is most reliable.

I told them I would bring them some cards shortly. As I attempted to side-step my way toward Russell, Tim McCoy threw his arms up in the air and right into one of the floor vase arrangements. Pink mums and lilies splayed around Sarah McCoy's feet. He bolted out of the room, not giving me so much as a glance. I could see him stomping down the hallway toward the men's room.

J.J. and Alex hurried into the Rose Room to pick up the vase. I looked up and saw Arthur Snugg peering out his office door, phone in hand. When he saw the twins working to clean up the mess, he nodded and went back into his office, closing the door.

"Her family is going to miss her," I said to Sarah McCoy, who was standing next to the casket and staring down at Stephanie.

"Tim, too." Sarah bent and removed a mum petal from her shoe.

"It's hard to lose an old friend," I said.

Sarah looked toward the hallway and the men's room door. Her expression turned sour, and anger radiated from her stare like Superman's heat vision.

"There she is," Don Gregor said in a voice barely audible above J.J. hand-vacuuming the water and green floral foam pieces that had fallen in the vase spill. "I'm so glad Stephanie had such a good friend. She is nothing like her mother," he said, his voice rising to make himself heard as he walked over and enveloped me in a fatherly hug. Sarah McCoy walked away.

Don Gregor thanked me repeatedly and introduced me to several of the people standing around. Russell walked over and gently took my arm. Russell and I took a few steps toward the hallway when Julie entered and waved at me like she was in a parade. She then went over and joined Lindsey Held, Dave Davis, Tim McCoy, who had returned from the men's room, Sarah McCoy, and Jake.

I wish Claire were here tonight to help gather intel.

Russell saw me looking and stopped. We stood silently, trying to look inconspicuous, as together we watched them. After a few minutes, the group came toward us like a pack.

"I will be over by the flowers," Russell said. "Within earshot," he whispered in my ear.

"Ask her. Here she is. Right here," Julie said.

Jake stood sheepishly behind everyone.

"I'm telling you, it's true!" Lindsey said to the pack.

"That might be true, but I'm telling you guys what Melody just told me a few minutes ago." Jake stepped forward, wiped at his eyes, and looked sadly at Stephanie.

So much for high school confidants.

"Melody, you sure seemed nervous the other day. Maybe you had something to do with her passing away." Tim's eyes narrowed.

"You were the last one to talk to her. Weren't you, Melody?" Julie asked. She opened her purse, removed a notepad, and began to jot notes.

"This isn't your chiropractic practice, so you don't need to take my history and physical like I'm a new patient."

Julie's cheeks puffed. She blew out a breath and pocketed her notepad.

"And, where were all of you on Friday afternoon?" I asked, looking from one now accusing face to the next. "I'm sure the police will be very interested to know." I projected my voice toward Russell.

"I have an alibi. Dave and I were at work, covering the pharmacy ourselves. Weren't we, sweetheart?" Lindsey squeezed her husband's arm.

Before Dave Davis had a chance to corroborate his wife's alibi, Tim McCoy piped in again, "She came snooping around our ice cream shop the other day."

"Whoa, hang on gang. Melody and Stephanie were friends, too. We all were friends." Jake put his hand on my shoulder. "She's upset too and is only trying to figure out what happened. You don't know for sure she was poisoned. Do you, Melody?" His gloomy blue eyes begged me to say no.

"How much do you think you know about your friend, Melody? She wasn't the saint you thought," Sarah bellowed as Tim wrapped his arm around his wife.

Dave Davis loudly cleared his throat.

"Sorry," Jake mouthed to me. He turned and slowly walked to the casket.

After the heated conversation with my old friends, the room cleared out. Most people left holding onto their significant other and quietly whispering.

At 7:50, the only remaining people were Stephanie's family, me, Lenny, and Jake. Mr. Snugg and the twins stood in the lobby, and Russell stationed himself at the doorway to the Rose Room.

After a short prayer service led by Lenny, all of Stephanie's family, except Don Gregor, tearfully departed.

"Melody, is it true what Jake informed us? You think perhaps someone poisoned Stephanie." Lenny pulled me aside and stood with his hands clasped together in front of him in the reserved pose that

Arthur Snugg uses when he is trying to remain calm while speaking to his twin nephews.

"I don't know. It's a possibility. Do you think Jake did something to her?" I looked toward Jake. He was standing silently with his hands on her casket.

"He loved her. Unfortunately, she never reciprocated that love," Lenny said.

Don Gregor came over, suit coat in hand.

"Pastor Blane, I can't thank you enough." He placed a sealed envelope in Lenny's hands. "For the church, Pastor."

Lenny shook Don Gregor's hand and called out to Jake.

"Ready to go?" Lenny asked, putting his arm on Jake's shoulder and leading him toward the door.

I watched them all leave together. Two heartbroken men and the one man's best friend, a minister. I wiped the stream of tears that suddenly flowed from my eyes and chewed and swallowed two mints.

As soon as they were out the door, Russell came over.

"Mel, after tonight, I can see it is futile to ask you to please let the police handle the investigation into Stephanie's death. I don't know whether to commend you for blowing everything wide open or to give you a warning about hampering my surveillance."

"I got them to talk."

"Yes, you certainly did." Russell's deep voice shook.

"I guess I've committed more than a rookie mistake."

"Clutch, I would say you've moved right into the major leagues by telling Jake and Lindsey your thoughts. Wasn't the break-in of your apartment warning enough?"

"If only I could figure out the heavy hitter in Stephanie's death." I looked toward her casket.

"If foul play is involved, you've given me some clues as to the starting lineup, that's for sure," Russell said.

"Tomorrow, you two will meet me here at 10:00 a.m. sharp," Arthur Snugg said to Alex and J.J. as they ambled down the staircase from Snugg's office. "We will lay Ms. Gregor to rest in the Garden of Peace." Snugg walked to my office, put paperwork on my desk, and went from room to room, shutting off lights. When the lobby was the only remaining light in the building, he returned to where Russell, Alex, J.J., and I were waiting.

"Melody, I expect you will be here tomorrow at 9:00 a.m."

We all filed silently out of the funeral home doors. Arthur Snugg locked the door, and Russell walked me to Blue Betty.

"I'll follow you home. You are going straight home, right?" Russell asked.

"Yes." I climbed in, closed my Jeep's door, and automatically turned on my windshield wipers. It cleared my view but not my thoughts.

Once home, Russell checked the surroundings, and after assuring him I was in for the evening, he gave me a soft kiss and headed back to work. I went straight to my wine cart and opened a bottle of Merlot. After pouring a glass and pacing around the room a few times, I sat down and redid my list from earlier, changing it slightly after tonight.

<u>My Top "Suspects"</u>

1. Tim McCoy and/or Sarah McCoy (These two take the sweetness out of ice cream, and it is becoming apparent that Tim had more contact with Stephanie than Sarah liked.)

2. Brandon Hoff and his soon-to-be wife, Rachel Grey (Where were they tonight? Perhaps it was time to play darts at their bar? They are suspicious. Maybe one of the bar owners decided it was "last call" for Stephanie. Which Hoff made the "off"?)

3. Lindsey Held (What would be her motive?)

4. Julie Paine (Could Stephanie have fallen out of alignment with this woman enough to make Julie want to harm her?)

5. Lenny Blane (Still at number five. A minister walks into a bar sounds like a party joke, but something isn't right.)

I called Claire.
"Hey, Mel...ody," Claire said mid-yawn.

I looked at the tabletop clock Arthur Snugg had given me as a gift for my first anniversary of working at the funeral home. "It's a family heirloom, runs like a charm, and is very dependable. It even lights up the dark. Just like you," Snugg said at the time. I laughed at Arthur Snugg's rare compliments and jokes. The clock read 9:40. Claire could never stay awake past 10:00.

"Claire, I need to tell you about Stephanie Gregor's service tonight."

"Oh, Melody, are you okay? I should have gone. But I'm glad I saw Morgan. He's so dreamy. We made plans for next week." Claire giggled like a young girl.

"That's great, Claire. Yeah, I'm okay. I think." I got up from my computer, walked into my bedroom, and lay across the bed.

"Melody, I don't know why, but I got a feeling you might be right about all of this with Stephanie. Morgan said that Rachel and Brandon were at the hotel earlier and they were arguing. He told them we helped him finalize the menu."

"Oh, great. Is there a C list that I am being moved to? Ha-ha."

"You haven't lost your sense of humor, that's for sure. Morgan feels so bad that he couldn't catch the person who broke into your place."

"How is Morgan? Did he say anything that might help me figure this all out?" I stretched over, opened the dresser drawer next to my bed, and pulled out a tablet and pen.

"No, but he is feeling better. He said something about the spinach helped. I don't know, but anyway, he appreciated me checking. I'm sorry I didn't go tonight."

"It's okay, Claire."

"Was Jake there?"

"Jake was there."

"Hold on a minute, Melody. I need to sit up and turn on the lights in my room. Better yet, I should keep them off. How did he look? Hot as ever?"

"Actually, Claire, Jake is going through some tough times." I took a deep breath.

"Man, that's a shame. Okay, dish on the others. Did anyone give you any info on Stephanie?"

"Well, Tim McCoy and his ice cream wife are cold."

"I just bought fudge ripple. It was on sale at *Shop Right*," Claire said brightly.

"I bought some last week. Missed the sale. But, Claire, they all sort of accused me of snooping around."

"Oh, Melody, that's horrible. I feel bad I wasn't there. Maybe we should cancel Friday night."

"No. I think we should go on as planned. Together we can gather intel."

We said good night, and I lay down in bed, pulling my pillow out from under my head and placing it over my eyes to block out the world.

Before I fell into a fitful, dream-filled night about Stephanie, I thought of Bernie, the little kitten I had fed at the police station. I wondered how he was doing at the shelter. I hoped the kitten was eating and adjusting.

Thursday morning, I awoke early and arrived at work at 8:40. After turning on every light, I walked into the Rose Room where Stephanie's now closed casket lay. On a nice day, the room has a window allowing in plenty of warming sunlight and offering a picturesque view of the eight-foot cross, which is the focal point in the Garden of Peace. Today, however, it was raining. I approached the casket and offered a prayer for her eternal rest and vowed again that although it seemed she certainly had a lot of frenemies in her life now, and, although I didn't know what brought her in search of me last week; I was going to do my best to find the answer. I wiped my eyes, blew my nose, and turned to leave. Alex stood in the doorway, eyeing me cautiously.

"Wow, this job is really getting to you," Alex said, walking toward me, a cup of coffee in his hand. "Sip it carefully, Mel," he said, handing the cup to me.

"Why?" I sputtered, nearly spilling the coffee on my bright floral swing dress and Snugg's carpeting.

"J.J. made it," Alex said, taking the cup from my hand. "Here, let me carry it to your office. Uncle A's red carpet doesn't need a caffeine fix."

"Hey, Mel, watch me walk so straight and tall," J.J. said as he strolled through the lobby, engaged in a balancing act of prayer cards on top of my new bronze cross shipment.

"If I had had brothers, I imagine them to be like you two guys." I walked into my office and turned on my computer.

"What does that mean?" Alex questioned.

"Thanks, sis," J.J. said, putting the prayer cards and cross boxes precariously teetering on the end of my desk. He stood tall in his 6'2" thin frame and ran his hand over his buzz-cut blondish hair. The box of prayer cards spilled onto the floor. "It wasn't me, Mom. It was Melody," he hollered as he ducked out of my office and jogged down the basement steps.

At 9:30, the door of the funeral home opened with a bang, and Arthur Snugg walked in. He shook off his raincoat and deposited his damp umbrella into one of the two umbrella holders/urns I placed in the lobby for days like today. Snugg's ex-wife, Regina Snugg, had purchased the urns shortly before leaving him. I heard from Alex that she joked about it being a parting gift to Snugg and his beloved funeral home. Two expensive, two-and-a-half-foot urns on the funeral home credit card. I tried to place them on display for purchase with the rest of the urn selection, but people kept putting their umbrellas into them, so I repurposed them into umbrella stands.

"Melody, I know how upset you have been over your friend. I thought of something that might make you feel better," Arthur Snugg said as he barreled into my office.

"I need something to make me feel better, Mr. Snugg, that's for sure." I smoothed out the Peter Pan collar on my swing dress and looked into the mirror I had strategically placed in my office to see down the steps to the lower level. Russell was proud when he saw it. He said, "You are something else, Melody Shore. No one will ever sneak up on you."

When I looked back at Snugg, he was watching me cautiously.

"Sorry, Mr. Snugg, you were saying." I sat up tall, picked up my notepad, and readied my pen.

"Melody, the angle on that mirror allows you to see down the steps to the lower level. Great idea." He looked at me with respect.

From the basement, the sound of loud music carried up the lower-level stairs. I could make out J.J. belting out his hip-hop rendition of "Singing in the Rain." Snugg turned toward his lobby and the umbrella-filled urn.

"Thanks, Mr. Snugg. I think we both know things aren't always peaceful here at The Peaceful Rest. It makes me feel better to see who is coming up the steps." I gave him a hopeful smile and put down the pen. "What did you want to tell me to make me feel better?"

"I don't know why I didn't talk to you about this before. Things have been busy." His voice trailed off as he looked toward the Rose Room and Stephanie's closed casket.

"You were saying, Mr. Snugg?"

"Yes." Snugg sat down in my spare office chair. "When your friend called to make the appointment, she asked if you were the manager here. I've thought about it. You have certainly proved yourself. You should have the title, Manager, or whatever you think appropriate."

"That's great, Mr. Snugg. Thank you. I have been meaning to talk…"

"Melody, it's a shame you didn't get to talk to your friend. We never know what is going on with another person. Seeing them in person and hearing their voice is the window to the soul."

"Stephanie's voice…Did she sound sick when she called?" My heart rate quickened. I stood up.

"No, I just meant that it would have been nice if you could have become reacquainted again." Snugg stood as well.

"When did she call to make the appointment?" I reached across my desk and scrolled through my computer messages. "How did she know I worked here?"

"I don't know, Melody, maybe a few days before. You were at lunch. I noted it on your desk calendar there." He pointed and sat back down. "We need to review that automatic calendar thingee you set up for us again." Snugg sighed. "Regina did everything on paper. I would like to learn."

"Sure thing, Mr. Snugg." I closed the computer program, sat back down, folded my hands, and waited for Snugg to speak. When he didn't, I said, "Did she say anything else?"

"No. Wait, she asked if you were involved with a police officer."

"Why would she want to know who I was involved with?" I shouted as I jumped up. My dress caught on the drawer of my file cabinet, and the drawer flew open.

Arthur Snugg slouched down in his chair. "Melody, I'm sorry. I was headed to see Ida and running late. I didn't give out your personal information. I simply said she could come and talk to you in person." He stood and moved into the office doorway. "I was telling you this to make you feel better, but it seems I have upset you again."

"No, wait, Mr. Snugg, did she say anything else?" I grabbed his arm and held it tight.

"She said you were always a team player."

"She did?" I paced my fishbowl office like a circling shark, stepping around Arthur Snugg, who stood fixed in my doorway. "She sought me out for a reason. Perhaps she knew someone was trying to harm her." I turned and walked in the opposite direction. "She wanted to tell me and ask me to inform Russell who could help her. But why didn't she go to the police herself? Because she did something illegal herself…That has to be it!" I sat back down at my desk, my fingers poised over the keyboard, waiting for Snugg to chime in.

Arthur Snugg sat back down. "You are quite the detective. Your father would have been proud. You'll figure it out." The color returned to Snugg's worried face. "I'm sorry you couldn't help her when she was alive, Melody."

Alex and J.J. silently walked by, pushing Stephanie's casket toward the elevator. Snugg nodded to the twins, straightened his tie, and turned his solemn funeral director's eyes to me. It was back to business at The Peaceful Rest.

"Now, if you feel up to it this morning, I could use your help, too. I would like to go over the paperwork you did with Don Gregor." He gave me a tight-lipped smile.

"Sure, Mr. Snugg." I pushed the drawer to my file cabinet back in, pulled the Gregor file from my "to-do" box, and handed it to him.

Snugg began to review the paperwork, only commenting every few minutes with a "hmm" as he paged through it.

"Perhaps we should remove the fee chart and instead list a descriptive paragraph. It allows for a bit more wiggle room with pricing." Arthur Snugg looked at me expectantly.

"Mr. Snugg, I don't think…"

"Melody, you are right. Why would I say that? It's been over a year since Regina left me. That is something she would say. Price gouger." He shook his head. "I'm a funeral director. I need to be celebrating. I need to start remembering why my grandfather started this place. Family," he said, smiling warmly at me and then looking sadly out toward the lobby and his family's photos. "As of today, I am putting Regina's old ways to rest." He sighed. "You did a great job, Melody, thank you. You have earned the title of Office Coordinator."

I fingered the edge of my "Why Snugg Needs Me and Doesn't Pay Me Enough" list. I had put it away in my drawer last week, but pulled it out this morning, contemplating speaking to Arthur Snugg.

Right now, my emotions are drained. But the title's a good start to advancing my place here at Old Peaceful.

"Thank you, Mr. Snugg. Oh, and speaking of celebrating, Ida Stoner phoned. She said she couldn't get you on your cell. She was wondering if you were free this evening. She was going to make you a special dinner at her house."

Snugg's eyes lit up. He reached into his pant pockets and then frantically searched his suit coat for his phone.

"Must have left my phone in the hearse when I stopped for gas this a.m." He hurried from my office and out to the hearse.

The rain gave way to sunshine, and the rest of the day went quickly, without incident. We had one new body arrive. Arthur Snugg spoke to the family and sent me an email from his office saying they would be in tomorrow to make arrangements, and he would handle everything. He requested that I put the appointment on the calendar for him.

The deceased was elderly. She had moved to Pleasantview several years back from Philadelphia. Her only son would be arriving tomorrow, traveling by motor home.

In the afternoon, I called Alex into my office.

"Do you and J.J. have dinner plans? Russell is working."

"You're inviting us to dinner? Wow, that must have been some coffee J.J. made you this morning."

Alex plopped down into my guest chair and put his feet up on my desk. "What gives?"

"I've been wanting to try this bar, and I heard they have a state-of-the-art dartboard."

"Oh, excellent! Sure, we're free."

"Don't you want to ask J.J.?"

"Nope, he'll be in. I'm sure."

"Great. One thing, though." I stood and knocked his feet down from my desk.

"We go Dutch?" he asked. He pulled out his wallet, shook it, and stared into the empty shell.

"I will treat, but here's the deal…" I stopped and gave him my best stern teacher look. "When I win at darts, and I will, you will no longer put your feet on my desk."

"You drive a hard bargain, Melody." He jumped up, put his hand out to shake, and then raced down the lower-level stairs to find J.J.

I took out the wipes and cleaned my desk.

What could go wrong with those two along?

When 4:00 came, I shut down my computer and forwarded all calls to Arthur Snugg.

I hadn't heard from Russell all day, so I called him.

His phone went straight to voicemail.

I sat at my desk, staring out of my office at the new red carpeting where Stephanie had collapsed.

Maybe this was a sign that I should get a new career.

Then I began to daydream. I imagined working with Russell at our own private detective agency. A small office with our names on the door. Working day-to-day together.

J.J. interrupted my thoughts.

"Hey, Sis."

I shivered as I came back to reality. J.J. jumped back from my office doorway and peered at me through the glass wall.

"Mel, are you okay?"

"Yes, you startled me. Just daydreaming, J.J."

"I have been standing here for like five minutes, calling your name. Are we going to dinner still? Cause my stomach has been growling for the past hour." He rubbed his stomach for effect and then lifted a case from the floor. It was shiny black and trimmed in neon green. Holding it up like a game show host displaying a prize, he twirled it around and then plunked it down on my desk.

"My dart case." J.J. opened the latch and began to remove the darts, fluffing the feathers and returning them to the case. "Ready?" he asked.

When we entered Hoff's Bar & Grill, Brandon was tending bar. He glanced my way, wiped his hands on a towel, and then pushed his way through a double door behind the bar. As he walked through, I could make out a small industrial kitchen area.

Where is he going? I need to question him and Rachel about Stephanie. With the twins here, I have safety in numbers.

J.J. and Alex rushed to a high-top table near the dartboard.

"Hey, Mel, we decided you get the winner," J.J. said, laying his darts out and then racing to the jukebox and playing *Eye of the Tiger*.

"Which will be me," Alex proclaimed proudly, pumping out his chest and cheering for himself.

"Let's all just throw to warm up." I picked up one of the darts, took aim, and threw. My shot landed on the edge of the bullseye.

"Melody needs a partner," J.J. announced loudly. He picked up one of his darts and eyed up the board before making a very good but not bullseye-worthy throw.

"I guess my games with Russell in the basement of the police station for the holiday party paid off." I took a bow and then looked towards the bar where Rachel Grey now stood. She eyed us with a puzzled face.

I want to get the two of them together before I start asking questions. One of them might say something to contradict the other.

As J.J. and I practiced, Alex went to the bar and came back with three bottles of beer.

"I started a tab. You are paying, right, Mel?" Alex popped the top off two beers and then handed one to me.

I threw another shot right into the bullseye. "I should have said loser buys."

"I ordered wings, they should be right up," Alex said.

"Can we add nachos?" J.J. asked.

After a winning round of darts, almost famous nachos, chicken wings with hot sauce, two more beers, and a neon pink cocktail appeared at the high-top table we were standing around.

"This must be for another table," I said, holding up the pink drink.

"They are on special tonight. It's called a 'pink lady.' We took care of your tab. This is on the house," Brandon said as he came up behind me.

I set the drink down and popped the top off one of the two beers. None of my male companions said a word.

"Hey, can I get another beer over here?" A guy dressed in a form-fitting t-shirt, washed-out jeans, and a baseball hat, tapped his empty beer on the bar's wooden top.

"Watch the game, Mark. You can't run a tab every night and not pay up. You're free beers have run out for tonight," Rachel said as she walked over to join us. "Melody, can we talk?"

"Here?" I asked, looking at Alex and J.J., who were chowing down on the nachos and wings.

"No, in the back," Rachel said, motioning toward the kitchen.

I glanced around. *There are probably loud appliances, knives, and numerous other things that could be used as weapons in the kitchen, and J.J. and Alex would only notice me gone when they ran out of food, which would be too late for me.*

"Here is good. What do you want to talk about?" I asked.

"Have you found out any more about Stephanie's death?" Brandon whispered.

Rachel was biting her lip and her eyebrow was twitching.

"Like, who did it?"

I wish Russell were here. Maybe I should have tried to question them alone. Divide and conquer.

"Yes, do you have any ideas? Because, Melody, I'm afraid I might be next. Whoever hurt Stephanie might come after me next." Rachel had a tight grip on Brandon's arm.

"Why would you say that, Rachel?"

"Our wedding is making people very upset," Brandon answered.

"Upset? Who?"

"Well, Rachel, for one. And Tim and Sarah. And, frankly, you too."

"I might be upset because you didn't invite me, but the real question is what happened to Stephanie. Rachel, why weren't you and Brandon at the funeral home last night?"

"I didn't think it would look good. You said there is an investigation. I thought the police would be there, and I was afraid. It doesn't look good for Brandon or me."

"Why wouldn't it look good for me? I didn't fight with her or threaten her. Oh, jeez." Brandon's six-foot body shrank a foot as he ducked and reached for his wife-to-be.

"Brandon!" Rachel elbowed her fiancé.

"I'm sorry this wedding is making me lose it." He touched the spot on his rib that Rachel had struck.

"What did you threaten her with, Rachel? You need to tell me," I said.

"Go on, Rach. Maybe Melody can help," Brandon said, rubbing his hands on his jeans.

"I told her I would put an end to her, but I didn't mean literally. I can't help that she ended up dead. I didn't kill her." Rachel crossed her arms in front of her and then rubbed her temples.

"Did this happen when you were at her house?" I asked.

Rachel froze.

"I know about the party last Thursday. You need to tell the truth."

"She invited me and Lindsey over. She went on and on about her new decorating gig. That's when I found out it was true what Brandon told me. She had received a boatload of money from the contract to decorate the hotel. She said her contractor would start immediately."

"Why was Lindsey there? I thought she wasn't close with Stephanie anymore?"

"Stephanie wanted Lindsey to sign on to redo the pharmacy, too."

That confirms what Lindsey said.

"Lindsey could just tell her no. She wasn't interested." I put down my beer and gave her a closed-lip smile.

"She did, but then Lindsey became furious with Stephanie when she brought up how she had already spoken to Dave about it, and he seemed to be on board. Melody, if someone hurt Stephanie, I'm worried I'm next." Rachel hugged herself.

I was the last one with Stephanie.

I dug into my purse and produced the paper I found at Stephanie's duplex.

"You think you're worried. This was found in her apartment with my name and phone number written down. I could be next."

"Let me see." Rachel held out her hand.

"Oh, I wrote that one day at the bar for her. She asked about you, and I wrote your number down. I have it here in my contacts." She produced her phone and scrolled to my name.

"Why do you have the Peaceful Rest's number?" I took the paper back and secured it in my bag.

"My mom gave it to me when your mom was still in her book club. She said your mom was always pushing funeral arrangements. Do you get a kickback or something?"

If I did, my mother would probably want a cut…but that is nice that she is promoting me and my new career.

"Back to Stephanie. I know she was at your bar the day she passed away." My hand flew up to my mouth. "I mean, was she at your bar last Friday afternoon?"

"Do the police know?" Rachel looked toward the bar entrance.

"Yes. And, I'm sure they will be talking to you soon." I picked up a nacho and then put it back down.

What if they tampered with our food?

I looked at J.J. and Alex. They were happily eating.

I will never forgive myself if I put them in harm's way.

I glared at Rachel. Brandon moved off to the side by the twins as Rachel and I continued our back-and-forth tennis match of words.

"Melody, I didn't hurt Stephanie. You have to know me. Sure, I was upset at Stephanie still trying to use her female charms and getting the guys to do what she wanted. But not enough to kill her." Rachel clasped her hands together as if begging me to believe her.

"Even if her contract to renovate the Admiral Hotel made it look like you were getting married at a construction site?"

"Yes. I mean, no. Look, we are having a really small wedding. It was going to be only family, but then we decided to include a few friends we still see."

"You don't still see Claire."

"Julie suggested we include Claire."

"Julie suggested you include Claire?" My mouth dropped open.

"Can I give you ladies my opinion?"

Rachel and I turned to face Brandon.

"If both of you stop for a minute. I just want to say, the last time you talked to Julie, remember you said she kept name dropping Claire? I think it's because she needed Claire's dress shop. Saves Julie money. You know, Rach, for that party she wanted to throw you." Brandon put his arm around Rachel.

"Brandon's right. I don't think her chiropractor business is making all the money she spends. Melody, you have to believe us."

I looked from Brandon to Rachel. At the moment, they both seemed sincere.

"But, I heard Claire has a fantastic clothing shop. I mean, Melody, I hope you come on Friday and the wedding." Rachel smiled for the first time at me since walking over to our table.

"You don't have to fake it; I saw my name on the 'B list.'"

I opened my purse and began to dig through it. At the bottom, almost forgotten in the past few days, I found the "B list." I pulled it out, unwrinkled it, and thrust the page at her and Brandon.

"What are you talking about?" Rachel took the paper from my hand. She stared at it silently for a moment and then repeated my words. "B list."

"Let me see that. Where did you get one of her honey-do Brandon lists?" Brandon took the paper from his bride-to-be's hands. "Yep, that's one of them."

"That was a list for you? The "B list" isn't a wedding invitee list. It's your list for Brandon. Why would you be giving a list to Brandon with mine and Stephanie's names on it?" My pulse quickened and I moved closer to Alex who was munching on nachos and staring at the bar's TV, which was showing a basketball game. He was oblivious to the conversation that me and my former friends were having. "What was he supposed to do to us? Or did he complete part of the list, and I was next?" My voice was shaking, and my stomach felt queasy. "I'm calling the police."

"Calm down, Melody. Please let me explain," Rachel said.

"It's not what you think," Brandon added.

"I made him that list as he is so good at talking to people. I tend to get upset quickly and blow up. I asked him to talk to Stephanie when I originally heard about the renovations. Before Thursday. I needed Brandon to make her understand this is our big day, sort of smooth things out." A tear escaped down Rachel's cheek. "Things really escalated."

"Escalated. Like how?" I grasped my beer bottle tightly.

"When he tried to talk to her, she went on and on about how she needed to start right away. Our wedding wasn't important to her. She said we would be in one of the rooms in the back and not even notice the scaffolding or demolished walls."

"Why was Brandon to talk to me?"

"Because when we invited Claire, I insisted you be invited too. But then, my mother didn't mail your invite because of her fight with your mother. She and I had it out about that, and I told him to bring you an invite and explain everything. He gave the invite to Stephanie." Rachel elbowed Brandon again.

"Stop it, Rachel. She told me she was going to see Melody and would do it for me. I thought I had won her over."

"So that's why she had an unopened invite. But, that doesn't explain why you both acted so suspicious and didn't explain anything when I showed up here on Saturday to tell you about Stephanie."

"I got scared when you said the police were investigating. I was afraid it would come out about how I had threatened her. I should have told you everything right then. I'm sorry I didn't. I would like you to come to the wedding if you want." Rachel looked at me with pleading eyes.

"I don't know, Rachel. I don't know if I believe any of this. Why aren't Lindsey and Dave coming to the wedding?"

"Because she is always worried about Dave cheating. From what I hear, they don't have a great relationship. She wouldn't have come to the wedding if Stephanie had come."

"Everything is out in the open now, Rachel. We have nothing to hide. Melody knows everything. We'll explain it to the police, and then we can move on and get married." Brandon hugged his fiancée tightly and they both looked expectantly at me.

"That's great. Can we get a few more beers?" J.J. asked, wiping the wing sauce from his mouth with a Hoff napkin.

"Melody, come on up to the bar, and let's finish talking. Rachel and I have to wait on our customers." Brandon gently attempted to guide me toward the bar.

"I need to think for a moment," I said, standing firm.

"Melody, please consider coming to the party on Friday. I think all of us together can make some sense of this. It might not be the party I hoped for, but it will be a good time to talk and heal." Rachel gave me a tight-lipped smile and then walked to the bar and began filling customers' drinks.

The bar's jukebox roared to life. Drunken Mark from the bar appeared behind me and whispered in my ear above the slow dance music, "Let's dance, pretty lady."

He grabbed my arm, and the next thing I knew, we were dancing. Actually, he was dancing, and I was dancing away from him.

Then it happened.

Drunken Mark became a little too friendly. He leaned forward and tried to kiss me. I stepped down hard on his leather-booted foot.

"Alex and J.J., let's go! Russell, my police officer boyfriend, is outside. Don't follow me or else," I said through gritted teeth to Mark.

"If Russell's here and you've got to go, we can get a bus, Mel. Thanks for everything," Alex said, moving toward the dartboard.

"See you tomorrow at work," the twins answered in unison as they both went back to their dart game.

Through the bar entrance walked Lenny Blane. I rushed at him, grabbed his arm, and pulled him out the door with me.

"Pastor Blane, walk me to my Jeep, please."

Lenny was about to protest when Mark came flying out the door after us.

"We need to go, now!" I said to Lenny.

When we reached Blue Betty, I opened the passenger side door and gently pushed Lenny in.

Then I ran around to my side, started my Jeep, and pulled away as Lenny tried to buckle his seatbelt.

"Melody, what are you doing?" he said mid-buckle.

"Listen, Lenny, confess to me now, what are you doing at the Hoff's bar? The day Stephanie passed away, and again tonight!" I slowed down, reached over and took the seatbelt from Lenny's hand and buckled him in.

"What was I doing there? What are you doing now?" he asked, turning to face me, his face blotchy red. "Besides accosting me!"

"I asked you first," I said, as I punched down hard on Blue Betty's gas pedal.

"Melody, I sell herbs and vegetables to Rachel. You saw some of my plants in my office. I also have a vegetable garden and some fruit trees. It is a way to provide a little extra income for the church. And, I am trying to help Jake. He needs a friend. Nothing more." He braced his hands on Blue Betty's dashboard as I maneuvered around a bend, not bothering to brake. "I was here last Friday and again today instead of tomorrow to deliver the produce order because I have a salsa competition tomorrow night and have to practice. I don't sell them much, but every little bit helps," he said breathlessly.

I bet Stephanie's groceries were from Lenny bringing them to the bar. Boy, do I feel like a fool. If Russell finds out that Stephanie wasn't poisoned and I have questioned and distrusted my old friends over this, my mother won't be the only one in Pleasantview with a reputation.

I slowed down and offered to drive Lenny home.

"Who will retrieve my car?" Lenny asked, his voice taking on a fire and brimstone preacher tone.

We drove back to the bar in silence.

"I am so sorry, Pastor Blane," I said as he got out of Blue Betty.

"Melody," he said, looking first at me and then upwards. "I have never said this before, but if you find yourself in need of a church, there are plenty of others around the area."

When I got home, Shady greeted me with extra love, rubbing around my legs and meowing softly.

After filling up his empty cat food bowl and standing watching him down his kibbles like it was his last meal, I sat down in front of my computer. Shady hopped onto my lap and did three circles and two kneading motions before settling in and allowing me to search the court record system online for Jake's name. He had a criminal record since high school: public intoxication, disorderly conduct, and three past DUIs.

That's probably why he wore the alcohol ankle monitoring bracelet and was entrusted to Pastor Lenny Blane.

I'm overthinking this whole thing. Tomorrow I will go to Claire's and apologize. Maybe we can have a nice night with old friends and maybe make a new one. Russell will figure out what happened, and I can put this whole thing behind me.

Shady meowed in approval.

Friday morning, Arthur Snugg arrived at his normal 10:00 a.m., dressed in a dark blue suit with a dark blue shirt. He whistled as he walked through the door of The Peaceful Rest.

"Good morning, Mr. Snugg. Did you get a new tie?" I asked as he pranced across his red carpet lobby. "I like the paisley orange print."

"Melody, my appointment for today is at 1:45. Please hold all my calls after they arrive," he said in a sing-song voice. "Oh, and Ida sent this salad from last evening for you." He walked into my office, reached into a shopping bag, and proudly produced two containers.

"This isn't just a salad, it was a work of art," I said as I opened the large, bright blue container with "Ida's Delights" etched on the side and peered at its contents. The bowl held a variety of fresh greens, romaine, endive, and arugula mixed with sprouts, plump ripe cherry tomatoes, beets, mushrooms, and cucumbers. The salad was sprinkled with fresh herbs, roasted walnuts, and grated cheese.

"She also insisted I bring you this accompaniment." Snugg handed me the smaller container. "It's her homemade ranch."

I was beginning to like Arthur Snugg's new friend. She was like my mom's best friend, Marsha. Ida greatly improved Snugg's mood. Marsha did her best with my mom's ever-changing moods. They were both a win for me because Ida and Marsha sent me food with no strings attached. My mother's food drop-offs always had an ulterior motive, and most of the time, it wasn't for my nutrition.

At the thought of my mom, my desk phone rang. Arthur Snugg walked out of my office and up the stairs to his.

"Melody, did you eat all the tuna casserole I brought over?"

"Mom, I don't need any more tuna noodle." My stomach growled.

I hadn't had time for anything but coffee and it's too early for Ida's salad.

I reached behind me and put the containers on my file cabinet.

"I told you I got a case on sale. Are you ever home?" my mother asked.

"You called me at work, Mom. Besides, even if I fed it to Shady and Russell and I ate it for every meal, I wouldn't finish it all. Listen, Mom, I have to get back to work. I promise I will call you tomorrow."

"Just call me tonight, dear. Around 4:30."

"No, Mom, I have plans tonight."

"Oh...anything you need company for?"

I hesitated.

What if there was foul play in Stephanie's death? Maybe I should tell my mother my thoughts.

For a brief second, I pictured her waiting for my signal, perched high on a pillow in Blue Betty. When I gave the signal, she would bust down the doors of Claire's Cottage screaming, "Whoever hurts my daughter answers to me." Yep, I might not want to admit it, but I share some of my mother's better characteristics.

"No, Mom, but thank you," I said, making a kissy chirping noise with my lips. "I'm sorry, but I have to get back to work."

"That Arthur Snugg. What is his hurry? Everyone there is dead. Bye, dear."

For lunch, I ate Ida Stoner's salad. Afterward, I phoned Claire and told her what Rachel and Brandon had said and about my Jeep ride with Lenny.

"So you don't think foul play now, and you are coming to the party and the wedding. Hooray," Claire said.

After speaking with my best friend, I felt reassured and energized. A short one-mile paved loop around the main quadrants of burial spots in the Garden of Peace would be a good day break and a chance to think. I retrieved my tennis shoes from the hall closet and laced them up.

As soon as I walked out the funeral home doors, I spotted a man dressed in jeans and a polo shirt standing in the Garden of Peace by Stephanie's grave. I was about 40 feet away. His back was to me, but I was close enough to tell it wasn't Alex or J.J. He had a very similar build to Tim McCoy.

I turned and walked in the opposite direction down an adjacent path.

If I can just get a look at his face, and that dimpled chin.

When I reached the bottom of the hill, I made a path straight up the back side of the slope. Cutting through the lawn, I came up directly behind a large statue. I crouched behind the statue.

From my vantage point, I could see it was Tim McCoy. He stood over Stephanie's newly excavated grave. For several minutes, he stood perfectly still, and then he lay a single flower down on the freshly mounded earth.

I looked down at my butterfly bangle watch. It was 1:30.

I have to get back to the office for Snugg's 1:45 appointment. I need to greet them.

I headed downhill, bringing me directly across from Stephanie's grave. When I got about 20 yards from where Tim stood, he turned and jogged toward the parking lot, where I could see an ice cream truck was parked.

Before he reached the parking lot, Tim stopped. He looked directly at me and then reached under his polo shirt.

I hit the ground and army-crawled over to a tombstone.

He has a gun! Mom always says, "Exercise will kill you." I should start taking her seriously. Why didn't I bring my phone? Where is he now?

My breath came out in shallow gasps. I peeked around the side of the tombstone. Tim was standing in the same spot, looking toward the row of markers where I was hiding. I ducked back down.

This ground planter is heavy enough to do some damage. If he comes close, I'm ready.

I pulled the carnations and daisies from the planter and then worked the whole thing out of the ground, sitting motionless, ready to strike.

I just need to hit him in the right spot...if he doesn't shoot me first.

I peeked back around the tombstone. A motor home pulled into the parking lot, and a man got out.

"There's ice cream here, Rose," the man's voice called out. "Sir, can I get two cones before we go in?"

I looked over the top of the tombstone. A thin, balding man walked around the motor home and opened the passenger door for a dark-haired woman who cautiously stepped out.

Arthur Snugg's 1:45 had arrived just in time to save me.

The woman spotted me and let out a scream. I ducked back down and peeked around the side of the stone.

"Johnathan, look over there!" She pointed my way. "A ghost just rose behind that tombstone."

"Rose, your active imagination is too much." The man put his arm around the woman.

"She's no ghost lady. She's a nosy old friend, and I'm not selling today," Tim hollered out.

He climbed into his white box truck with ice cream cones painted on the side and raced the truck out onto Republic Street. Ice cream music blared from the roof-mounted speaker.

I jumped up from the grass, dusted myself off, and hurried toward Snugg's appointment.

"You saved my…" I stopped.

These people will think I'm crazy if I say the ice cream man who just left was going to shoot at me. They probably think I'm a jolted girlfriend, and they interrupted a weird game of tombstone tag. The wife is still looking at me like I am the walking dead.

"Hi, welcome to The Peaceful Rest." I extended my hand.

The woman and man both stepped backward.

I looked down. My hands had mud caked on them and my pink and yellow striped midi dress had streaks of brown across the front from my belly crawl.

"Sorry, I work here. I was fixing the grave over there, and I guess I got carried away."

The woman took a few more steps backward, and the man said, "We are here to see Arthur Snugg. We can wait here. Please go get him."

"Let me take you inside the funeral home to Arthur Snugg, the funeral director. Sorry, he doesn't do business out on the lawn." I walked in front of them, motioning for them to follow.

Once I had Snugg's appointment in his office, and I was back downstairs, I put on my button-up, peach, knee-length sweater to hide the dirt stains. Then, I called Alex.

"Can either you or J.J. come see me?"

"J.J.'s is just headed out to trim grass around the tombstones, but I can come, sure," Alex said.

Two minutes later, Alex plopped down in my spare office chair and opened up a gaming magazine.

At least I have company if Tim returns.

I busied myself paying bills.

Ten minutes later, the couple that had saved my life came hurriedly down the stairs and exited the funeral home with only a short "Let's get out of here" goodbye.

Arthur Snugg stomped downstairs at 2:25, briefcase and suit coat in hand. He stepped into my office and handed me a piece of paper.

"No viewing, just burial," he said curtly. Snugg gave me an inquisitive look and continued, "That's the first time I have been asked to not let the dirty girl near the deceased." He turned his stern gaze to Alex. "Normally, it is you or your brother who causes all the malarkey."

"Whose your favorite now, Uncle A?" Alex got up and did a quick wobble dance move.

I glanced over the one-page paperwork. When no explanation for my behavior came to mind, I said, "When should I schedule the burial?"

"I am headed over to pick up Ida. I will prepare Ms. Stone tomorrow and the boys can handle everything on Monday." Arthur Snugg turned toward Alex, who nodded in agreement. Snugg checked his trusty Timex and said to me, "Melody, I want you to get some rest this weekend. Please."

"I will, Mr. Snugg. For sure!" I spun my chair around and carefully laid the paper in my "Needs Immediate Attention" bin on my file cabinet.

"Alex, you and J.J. prepare the grave site today and keep an eye on Melody," Snugg said to his nephew as he exited my office.

Two minutes later, after straightening his tie in the large lobby mirror, Arthur Snugg silently exited through the funeral home's front door. I watched out the window as the hearse pulled out onto Republic Street.

"Mel, I better find J.J. and get to work." Alex stood up and put his magazine under his arm. "But, if you need us for anything, we will be right outside. Okay?"

"Sure, if you have to. I understand. I'll be fine here, myself." I looked in my desk mirror. My eyes were watery.

"Mel, my dates don't even want me around this much. If we are going to date, I'll need to tell J.J., and you need to break it off with Russell." He gave me a mischievous smile.

"I appreciate your concern." I stood and elbowed him in the stomach.

"Ouch," Alex said, crouching over and holding his abs. Then he stood tall and said, "That's my Melody! And not that I am keeping score, but that's twice this week that you have got me in the ribs. Save it for the bad guys."

The outfit I picked for the fashion show was the Bordeaux polka dot dress. I decided to accent it with a thin silver chain necklace.

I called Claire, and while I told her about Tim coming to the cemetery, I scooped a small amount of fudge ripple ice cream into a bowl. The party wasn't until 7:00, and I needed a little snack to hold me over.

"First, you thought one of the Hoffs made the 'off', now you think it's Tim. Melody, no one poisons ice cream. It's just wrong." Claire nervously laughed at her joke.

"If it comes up, I'm going to apologize to Rachel tonight." I picked up my hobo bag and hugged it to my side. "Can you talk to Sarah and Julie?"

"About Tim?"

"No. I don't think we should tell Sarah that her husband was visiting the cemetery. Just try and make them understand why I acted the way I did at the funeral home, etc."

"Oh. Sure. I'm glad you are coming tonight, Melody. I called Lindsey and invited her too. I can't let Julie dictate the guest list. It's my party."

"Claire, did I tell you that Rachel said Lindsey was really mad at Stephanie as well?"

"No. But, I thought you were done thinking someone caused foul play with Stephanie."

"I'm just thinking, Lindsey is a pharmacist. She and her husband have access to all kinds of poisons."

"Yikes. I never thought about that. Melody, have you talked to Russell?"

"No, I called him, but he was in a meeting. He will be upset that I didn't immediately tell him about the Tim tombstone incident."

"But you really don't know if he actually had a gun, do you?"

"No. Now that I am away from the situation, maybe it was a cellphone."

"I wish the labs would come back," Claire said.

"Me too. I need to call Russell and tell him about Tim."

I hung up my phone and was ready to dial Russell when it began to ring.

Not a number I recognize.

"Melody, it's me," a voice whispered.

"Mr. Snugg?"

Shady jumped from his chair perch and knocked my ice cream spoon and bowl over. Ice cream splashed onto my dress.

"Shady!" I screamed.

Shady took off for my living room, and I could see his eyes peering from under the couch.

"What happened?" Mr. Snugg asked.

I rushed to the bathroom sink, ran cold water onto a towel, and blotted out the stain.

"Melody?"

"Sorry, Mr. Snugg. But why are you whispering and calling from a different number?"

"Melody, I left my phone at the funeral home."

"I'm sorry, but what does this have to do with me, Mr. Snugg?" In the bathroom mirror, I reexamined my splotched dress and hair.

"I was hoping if you were headed out, you know, to Russell's or somewhere, you could stop and check."

"The funeral home?"

Shady cautiously came over to me and rubbed around my legs.

"Yes. I would go myself, but Ida has prepared this fabulous dinner which will be ready any minute. I tried calling my nephews. Their phone goes to voicemail. I wouldn't ask, but as a funeral director, now that I have a phone, I am never without it."

"Did you check your suitcoat or car, Mr. Snugg? Remember, you left it in the hearse the other day?"

"I did, and I tried calling it. I hope I didn't drop it when Ida and I went bike riding this afternoon."

The thought of Arthur Snugg and his new girlfriend bike riding made me smile.

I stood in front of my full-length mirror, watching my chest turn to a shade of nervous red, wondering how I could help Snugg and still make the fashion show.

Coming back home was the best thing that could have happened to me. Like Claire, Arthur Snugg and the twins were family. If he needed me, I would somehow help him and still go to the party.

"If you aren't going out, I can leave Ida's and drive to the funeral home. I just thought I would ask," Snugg said, his voice breaking through my thoughts.

"No, Mr. Snugg, I would be happy to check and even bring it to you, if it's there. I caused a good bit of worry today with the way I acted around the deceased's family. I need to make it up to you." I walked back to the kitchen and picked up a pen and tablet lying on my table. "What is Ida's address?"

After Snugg gave me the address and hung up, I put it into my computer and mapped my way from the funeral home to Ida's.

I grabbed a light cotton, cream-colored sweater from my closet, and giving Shady a few head and neck rubs, I locked my apartment and headed out in Blue Betty.

When I pulled into the funeral home parking lot, it was empty and all the lights in The Peaceful Rest were off except the two small lamps set on a timer in the lobby window. J.J. and Alex had long gone home and were probably at a bar enjoying their Friday night.

I jumped out of my Jeep, unlocked the funeral home doors, turned on the stair lighting, and swiftly walked up the mahogany staircase. My strappy brown sandals made a clicking noise with each step. Arthur Snugg's heavy, closed office door sprung open with a rattle of the knob and a firm push. When I turned on the light, his flip phone lay smack in the middle of his immaculate desk. I picked up the phone, shut out the light, and headed back down the steps. I was about to leave the funeral home when I spotted Ida's salad bowl still lying on my desk.

I wanted to bring the bowl home and fill it with a sweet treat for Ida. My run-in with Tim killed that idea.

My mom's voice echoed in my thoughts, "Never return an empty bowl empty."

Does filling it with Arthur Snugg's mints count?

I grabbed the bowl and hurriedly filled it with the extra stash of mints I keep in my drawer for an emergency mint need. Before stepping out of my office, I glanced in the mirror I had strategically placed to see the lower-level steps.

"Ahh!" My scream echoed through the silent funeral home. My heartbeat pulsated into my ears as I ran. I was halfway across the lobby when I looked back toward the steps.

"Oh my gosh! It's only Alex's suit jacket draped over the banister."

I rushed back, grabbed the suit coat, and tossed it on my office chair. Then, I raced back across the lobby, flung open the door, and hurriedly locked the funeral home back up. I didn't slow down until I reached my Jeep.

I'm more nervous about tonight than I thought. I need to phone Russell.

Russell's phone went straight to voicemail.

"Russell, I will be at Claire's tonight for a party with my old friends. Could you send Kenneth over to patrol the area? I mean, if he is free. Just in case. I love you."

According to my GPS, Ida Stoner's farm sat four miles outside of Pleasantview.

I turned off Route 50 and steered Blue Betty along a dirt road, dodging road ruts and fallen tree branches. A small squirrel ran across the road and I braked for it. After a quarter-mile, a road sign directed me to Ida Drive.

Blue Betty's tires crunched along as I drove up the limestone driveway. At the top of the drive sat a picturesque country farm. A big orange tabby cat walked across the cobblestone walkway and lay down in the late afternoon sun. A brown horse grazed in a small red barn to the left of Ida's Victorian home. Large hanging baskets overflowing with cascading flowers hung off the home's wrap-around porch. On the porch was a recliner swing.

Snugg and Ida sat happily perched on the swing nestled amongst throw pillows.

"Mr. Snugg, I have your cellphone," I said as I climbed up the washed-out gray steps of Ida's home. Painted wisteria vines decorated each step and the porch's railings.

"Melody, why are you so dressed up?" Arthur Snugg rose and walked around me, taking in every detail.

"Arthur, she looks beautiful. You look beautiful, Melody," Ida Stoner said.

Arthur Snugg cleared his throat. "Melody, you look exquisite." He sat back on the swing and put his arm around Ida.

"Arthur, you asked this dear girl to come all the way here with your phone. I told you we could go look for it after dinner." Ida patted Snugg's leg.

"Thank you, Melody," Snugg said, taking the phone from my outstretched hand. "Any missed calls?" Snugg pressed a few buttons and lay the phone next to him on a small outdoor table before returning to swinging.

A dark storm cloud moved overhead, and I could hear a rumble of thunder in the distance.

"Maybe you better put that in the house, Arthur," Ida said, pointing at the darkening blue and orange sky. "We might get rain later tonight. I would hate for you to forget where you left it again."

Snugg picked up his phone and dutifully disappeared into Ida Stoner's house.

"Oh, here's your bowl too, Ida." I held the bowl out to her. "Your salad was delicious."

"Thank you, Melody. And I'm sorry you made a trip for Arthur all the way out here."

"No problem, really." I took a deep breath in.

"Melody, I can warm you up some dinner. It won't take but a minute." Ida got down from the swing and started across her porch.

"No, thank you. I have plans tonight."

"Oh, silly me, I forgot it's Friday night. Of course, you do. You probably have a date." Ida Stoner's eyes twinkled with mischief as she walked back toward me. "Can I at least cut the cake that I made? Maybe your date would like a piece?"

"No, thank you though, Ida." My stomach churned disapprovingly at my rejection of the cake. "Your farm is really beautiful." I looked out across the porch into the large flower field that stretched to the side of her home.

"Come on, just for a minute, let me show you around." She took my arm and gently pulled me down her steps and across the cobblestone to her flower beds. "If you like, you are welcome to return when you have time and dig into my dirt. I would love your company."

"Ida, your flowers are so pretty," I said as we strolled together down a path that wove through her gardens.

Ida Stoner had quite the green thumb. Delicate daisies grew next to black-eyed susan in harmony. Purple cone flowers reached their thin stalks skyward as feather reed grass rustled slightly in the breeze. Golden Rod clustered together at the border, framing the back of each carefully planted bed. I bent down to read a hand-painted sign that read "Ida's Summer Dream." Each garden had a different name, and every flower's name was displayed on separate wooden signs that hung from planters, decorative gnome figures, and painted posts.

I stopped in front of an out-of-place fenced-in plant.

"Why do you have a fence around that plant?" I asked as I stared between the steel poles that kept me from meandering toward the beautiful, cascading pink flower.

"That is an Angel Trumpet, dear."

"Oh, what a beautiful name." I reached toward the plant.

"Yes, very beautiful, but very poisonous."

My hand retracted faster than a game of hot hands.

"I can't have anyone touching it, hence the fencing." She patted my arm.

"Why do you grow such a thing?"

"My husband, before he passed away, got the plant from the minister of our church." She looked wistfully upwards. "He loved the name and the beautiful flowers."

"But, it's poisonous."

"When he told me how poisonous it was, I immediately told him I wanted no such plant growing on our farm. Sadly, he passed away, and my son hasn't had time to remove it. He is so busy working now at the church." Ida pointed at the plant. "Darn thing blooms every year around this time. The real name is Brugmansia."

Ida took her watering can and, turning away from the plant, carefully walked up and down her garden path, sprinkling the border of bonanza marigolds that framed the path.

"Wait, Ida, you said your son works at a church?"

"Yes, dear, why?"

Oh my gosh! I saw the same plant at the church where Lenny Blane is pastor! Ben told me about it. Oh, no, I pray Lenny didn't cause Stephanie harm. Wait, didn't Jake say that Stephanie had a salad that contained flowers? And, she put one in her hair.

"Yikes!"

"What, dear?" Ida asked.

"Ida, what's the minister's name?"

"I call him Pastor ~~Blane~~. Leonard is his first name." Ida stopped sprinkling her plants and walked over to me. "Why?"

"Is your son Ben?"

"Yes, he is. Do you know him?"

"I do. *And Lenny Blane.*

I opened the dial cover on my butterfly leather strap watch to reveal the time. It was 6:15. The party started in forty-five minutes.

"Ida, I'm sorry, I have to go now!"

"Of course, of course, Melody. Who are me and Arthur to hold up fate? Go on, we can chat about gardening the next time you come to visit."

I dashed back to Arthur Snugg.

"Mr. Snugg, I really should be going."

"Of course," Arthur Snugg said to me. He patted the seat next to him on the swing for his new love to join him.

Snugg and Ida returned to happily swinging on the porch, unaware of the fear Ida had stirred in me.

I pulled out of her driveway and gunned it down the dirt road and back to Route 50. My mind and Blue Betty were racing.

I tried to phone Russell. My call again went to voicemail. My voice shook as I left a message.

"Russell, please call me back."

I started to hypothesize out loud.

"Lenny poisoned Stephanie. Why? For Jake? Did Jake do it to get back at Stephanie? Why?" I swallowed hard as I steered around a sharp bend in the road.

A car passed me, the driver flicking her cigarette butt out the window. "Litterbug," I hollered. I slowed the car to the posted speed and drove to Claire's. My mind might be racing, but Blue Betty had to follow the speed limit.

I arrived at Claire's Cottage at 6:40. There was a spot right in front of the store, but I drove by and down a side street. Normally, I would park close, go right in, and see if Claire needed any help. After what just happened, I was back on the case. In the old detective shows I watch, the murder happens because of love, money, or revenge. I had investigated all the suspects I suspected but there had to be something I was missing. "Think, think," I muttered to myself as I parallel-parked Blue Betty. I pulled my hair up into a bun and tucked it under a floppy hat that I kept in my car for sunny days. Next, I put on my red sunglasses. I was in surveillance mode. With a quick check in my rearview mirror for support, I jumped out of my Jeep and hurried across the street. Diagonally across from Claire's was a garden center. I grabbed a shopping cart and picked up a pansy plant to look the part of a shopper. The pansy's yellow and black vibrant petals gleamed from a recent watering in the late day sun.

"Can I help you find anything?" A tall teenage guy with dark brown hair cut in a slicked-back undercut hairstyle stood looking expectantly at me. He was dressed in a t-shirt that said "Gerry's Garden Center - where sunshine and flowers are a way of life." I stared first at his hair. *Russell would look so sharp with that cut.* And then, I looked at his shirt. *What would I do if Snugg required us to wear uniforms? What would they say? 'The Peaceful Rest. Your death is our life.'* I shook my head. *That is something the twins would say. Spending so much time with them is wearing off on me.*

"That's an annual, not a perennial, you know," the guy said, breaking me out of my thoughts. He was pointing at the pansy plant in my hand.

"Oh yeah. Thanks. No, I think I'm good. Just snooping…I mean browsing."

"Uh, okay. I guess." He gave me a weird look and was about to walk away when a woman in a parked car said, "David, grab me a couple of snapdragons before you're done. You don't see that orange color much."

"Okay, Mom," he said. Then he turned to me. "We close in ten minutes." He picked up two orange snapdragons and headed into the store.

I looked down at my butterfly bangle watch. It was almost 6:50. I hoped the women would arrive early. I only had ten minutes to snoop and shop.

I had just picked up a container of snapdragons for my mom, too, when I heard laughter. I moved behind a large metal cart of vegetables. As I peered between the tomato plants, I could see Rachel and Julie walking up Fifth Street toward Claire's. Neither Lindsey nor Sarah was with them.

Rachel wore a thigh-length white sundress and carried a mint green purse. Julie had on a black tennis skirt and a pink polo shirt. Julie arrived at the door first and pulled it open.

The soundtrack music to *The Queen of Sheeba* played in my head as I watched Rachel glide past her through the entryway.

I should go over there and help Claire. I'm not going to learn anything over here.

I stepped from behind the vegetable cart and looked down at my dress and tan Mary Janes. I was wearing the same Mary Janes when Stephanie passed away at my feet. A lump formed in my throat, and tears began to well in my eyes. I put the pansy back, picked up a container of hens and chicks, and headed into the store to pay for my purchases. My mom will appreciate the gesture of snapdragons.

"Allergies," I said to the teen as I wiped a straggler tear that was cascading down my cheek. He ignored me and stood silently waiting. I handed him the plant payment, picked up the bag of plants, and was ready to walk across the street when I saw Lindsey and Sarah approaching Claire's Cottage.

Lindsey was dressed in bell-bottom blue pants and a light blue blouse. Sarah had on jeans and a hot pink shirt with what looked like little ice cream cones on it. Lindsey looked up and down the street, and then they both hurriedly went into Claire's.

Well, I learned nothing from that, but I did get some plants.

I ran across the street to join them.

I could hear laughter and music coming from my friend's store. With only a slight hesitation, I pulled open the flower-painted, frosted glass door and stepped in.

"I told you Claire has a beautiful shop," Julie said, waving her arms around, and then her arm came to rest on Claire's shoulder.

All five women turned as I stepped through the door.

Claire's tiny store was decorated to the hilt. She had moved her large glass mirrors from the dressing room out to her main area and created a stage. Strings of fake rose vines cascaded over the mirrors. Claire always had twinkle lights strung throughout the store, but today they were sparkling more because of the added mirrors in the room. Normally, she had a bargain rack front and center, but today, in its place, a table covered with a lace and rose tablecloth. On the table sat a champagne punch bowl, strawberries, and crystal glass flutes. Next to the drink display was a board filled with cheeses, crackers, and dips.

"Melody's here," Claire said, rushing over to greet me. She peeked into the brown bag I was carrying, and when she saw the plants, she smiled.

"I was a few minutes early, so I did a little plant shopping." I set the bag down by the door. "Everything looks great," I said, giving her a tight-lipped smile and nodding my head. "Thanks for including me. Hi everyone."

"Melody, I'm glad you came," Rachel said.

"Yay, Melody's here. Now the party begins," Julie said, sitting down and motioning for me to take a seat next to her on one of the four pink striped hassocks that Claire had in her shop.

"Yes. Let the party begin." Claire turned her door "Fashions Await" sign to "You Missed a Bargain." She locked the door and closed the blinds.

"What can I get everyone to drink?" Claire asked.

"Champagne, of course," Julie said, jumping up to help Claire. While the rest of us headed to the cheese and crackers, Claire and Julie filled five flutes with champagne and handed them out.

"I think you'll like it, Melody," Claire said. "It's not really dry."

"I picked it. Claire liked it when I brought her a bottle last week," Julie said.

Once everyone had a drink in hand, Claire looked at our old friends and raised her glass.

"To Stephanie. We will never forget you. Old friendships die hard, but we never expect old friends to die so young. Rest in peace, friend."

The women clinked their glasses, and the sipping and eating began. The conversation turned to Claire's store and how she had an eye for fashion.

"I can't wait to try that on." Rachel pointed to the white skirt and aqua blouse that Claire had promised I could have if I liked.

"Oh, that's not for sale," Claire quickly said. She turned and gave me a big smile.

"Why do you have items that aren't for sale hanging for display then?" Rachel asked, her voice taking on a sharp tone.

"Well, it was for sale, but it has been purchased. I took it out of the window, but didn't have time to take it off the mannequin," Claire answered.

"I'll go first," Julie said, jumping up and pointing to a blue jumpsuit that hung from a high rack. Claire picked up her clothes retriever pole, and got it down. She checked the size and handed it to Julie, who ran to the dressing room to try it on.

Once several outfits were tried on and opinions were given, Rachel began to dance, and everyone joined in.

"This reminds me of our slumber party days," Lindsey said, forgoing the dressing room and pulling off her shirt to try on a long swing dress.

The tone in the room changed to loud laughter and silliness. Claire turned up the music, and the women began trying on outfits one after another. If it wasn't their size, they were handing the item off to another person. Everyone had a stack of clothing and accessories next to them that they intended to purchase.

I turned toward Claire. Her eyes were sparkling as she looked at the piles of clothing each woman intended to purchase.

"This is a success. I might just be able to buy more boots," Claire whispered as she kicked up her heels.

"Thanks again for including me," I whispered back when she danced by.

About ten minutes later, Lindsey pulled open the blinds and looked out onto Fifth Street.

"Is there a lot of crime in this area?" she asked.

"Just fashion crime. Can I get anyone another drink?" Claire asked.

"I'll take care of the drinks and refill the food. You haven't tried on anything all night, Claire. Show us what you would put together," Sarah said.

"Yeah, it's your turn," the other women said in unison.

"Let's make this fun. A competition between old friends. I'll be the judge since I'm the newbie. Everyone has two minutes to create an outfit," Sarah said.

"Yeah, the winner gets a free massage from the new cute guy I just hired." Julie giggled.

"I'm taken, but what the heck. It's therapeutic and I've heard that chiropractors give the best massages," Lindsey said.

"I'm available for a few more hours," Rachel said.

"Start the clock," Claire said.

Lindsey, Rachel, Julie, Claire, and I hurried around Claire's Cottage picking through clothing.

As I rushed around Claire's store, I saw out of the corner of my eye a scarf that would look perfect with the blouse I had chosen. It was silk and had tiny roses on it. I picked it up and when I turned, that is when I saw Sarah put something in the glass that sat by my pile of clothing.

"What are you doing?" I asked, foregoing my outfit search and walking over to Sarah.

No one could hear me over the music.

"I saw you put something from that vile into my drink," I said, grabbing Sarah's arm.

She dropped her arm down, and the vile fell to the ground. Sarah kicked it under Claire's velvet couch.

"What are you talking about? I'm just waiting for you to go change," Sarah said, pushing me toward the dressing room.

I was about to drop to the floor to search for the vile when Sarah advanced toward me. I grabbed the closest thing to me, the broken arm from Claire's mannequin, and pointed it at her.

Claire, Rachel, Lindsey, and Julie excitedly ran over.

"Is time up?" Julie asked.

"Melody, what is going on?" Claire asked when she saw me literally armed with her mannequin.

"Are you going to fight?" Rachel shrieked.

"Melody, are you on drugs?" Lindsey asked.

"I knew I should have given you a deep tissue massage. Melody, you are too uptight," Julie said, flexing her fingers in a massage-like motion.

"Claire, call Russell, now!" I shouted above the dance music.

"You came in here and ruined everything," Sarah screamed. She grabbed her purse and pulled out a small knife. She sprang at me, missing and knocking into the drink table. The champagne began to flow, and not in a good way. It ran down the table and onto the floor.

Claire rushed toward the table and slipped on the wet floor.

Sarah lunged forward at me but missed and instead slashed a dress with her knife.

"If only short dresses were in," I said with a burst of bravery.

When she lunged again, I ran and grabbed the clothes retriever that Claire had used earlier and swung it like a baseball bat, striking her arm. The knife flew from her hand and skidded across the wet floor straight to Rachel, who picked it up and stood screaming in hysterics.

Sarah ran to the locked door and pulled on it. When it wouldn't open, she turned and fled into Claire's store. As she ran around the store, she threw clothing behind her and then directly at me in an attempt to block my path to catch her. I swatted away a cocktail dress, a nautical romper, and a velvet and paisley jacket before gaining speed and putting myself within arm's length. When she dashed to the back of the store, I was directly behind her. I scooped up a discarded maxi dress, flung it over her head, and pushed her into the dressing room screaming, "Try that on for size." Throwing my weight against the door I jammed the fingers from the broken mannequin arm between the door knob and the wall. Then I secured it with the scarf. Even if Sarah tried to open the door, she couldn't. She was locked in. Claire ran and opened her front door.

Rachel sat crying on the hassock as Julie massaged her shoulders. Lindsey paced the room twisting her wedding ring, and Claire and I were on the ground pointing to the vile of poison that Sarah had attempted to use when Russell and Kenneth burst through the door.

"Mel, I got your message, and the lab results are back. Someone poisoned Stephanie. She had antifreeze in her system."

Claire and I stood up and pointed under her velvet couch. Glove-clad Kenneth bent down and picked up the vile. From the dressing room came loud banging. Russell cautiously approached, gun drawn. When he saw the mannequin arm wedged in the door, he laughed out loud.

"Let me guess, you caught Stephanie's killer?"

"You knew I would."

Russell unwound the scarf and opened the door.

Sarah stood with her hands on her hips in the dressing room. When she saw Russell and Kenneth with guns drawn, she began to murmur.

"I had to get her out of the way," she said.

"Why did you do it, Sarah? Why did you kill Stephanie?" I asked, shielded behind Russell and Kenneth.

"We borrowed from Tim's dad to buy the ice cream shop. We're way over our heads. I told Tim and his dad I could handle the hotel renovations. Me! The hotel could pay me. But Tim's dad said no way. I had no decorating education, and he had already given us too much money."

"Why would Tim pay Stephanie then?" I asked.

"He didn't. His dad paid her for the hotel and his new restaurant, The Artisan. I know his father wished Tim had married her. He brought Stephanie up a lot." Sarah began to clench and unclench her fists.

"So you poisoned her?"

"When I saw her at the bar Friday, I gave her pink drink a little more flavor. You have to understand, she was destroying my life. I went to her duplex Wednesday night to tell her I would be handling the hotel remodel. She just laughed and told me to do what I do best, scoop ice cream. That hotel is going to be mine and Tim's one day. Mine and Tim's!"

"Were you going to poison me, too?"

"Just a little to warn you. Make you sick. You kept snooping around. I thought breaking into your apartment would scare you enough to stop, but you didn't. You just didn't stop."

"What's in the vile?"

"Antifreeze."

Kenneth snapped handcuffs on Sarah.

As Kenneth led Sarah out to the waiting squad car, Russell turned to me.

"Okay, Ms. Private Eye, I need to know your answer."

"What's the question?" I asked, staring up into his deep brown eyes.

"Was it money, love, or revenge that motivated this crime?" Russell asked with a grin on his face.

"I think in Sarah McCoy's case, it was all the above." I melted into Russell's arms and kissed him passionately.

A week later, Russell, Claire, and I were at my apartment discussing Rachel and Brandon's wedding. In front of us lay a smorgasbord of sauce-flavored wings.

"It sure was a nice wedding, even after everything that happened," Claire said.

"Everyone liked your choice of keeping the bar open during dinner." Russell popped the tops off of two beers and handed Claire and me each one.

"I feel bad for Tim. He's going to have it rough for a long while." I stared at my framed pictures of Pittsburgh. "It's good he has his family to fall back on."

The conversation then turned to Sarah McCoy.

"Once we got a full confession, she admitted breaking into Stephanie's duplex and stealing the money for the hotel renovations." Russell twisted the cap off a beer for himself.

"And, they searched the ice cream shop and found my bricks. Good thing I mark them with nail polish."

"Sounds like the only thing she will be serving is hard time," Claire said, taking a bite of a wing. "Oh, I almost forgot, Julie called yesterday and said to tell you hello. She also had an update on Jake. He rented a room across from the church, and he's working for the new construction company Tim's dad hired to renovate. Turns out Jake is one heck of a carpenter. I mean, wasn't that trellis beautiful he made for the wedding?" Claire wiped wing sauce from her mouth.

"It sure was. Hopefully, things will improve for him in all aspects of his life with friends' help." I looked lovingly at Claire and Russell. "Dinner this Friday? Russell works, and we haven't done an E&R night in a while."

"I love our Eat and Recap nights and we can go to my store after. I promised you a fun shopping spree, and I always keep my word and my boots." Claire kicked her leg out, showing off her sapphire, blue leather boots she had purchased from Julie's shopping spree.

"How about the Corner Cupboard?" I asked.

The Corner Cupboard is Claire, mine, and Russell's favorite diner on the corner of Main and 5th Street, in the center of Pleasantview. They served salty fries, juicy hamburgers, and spicy gossip if you sat at the bar during happy hour. This Friday, we had enough gossip to keep Claire and me talking for the whole evening.

"It's a date. Oh, I also didn't tell you guys that Morgan and I are planning on going to Pittsburgh. He wants to take me on that ship, *The Gateway Clipper*." Claire's voice oozed with happiness.

Claire and I clinked our beers together as a knock could be heard at my door.

Russell got up and opened my locked door. My mother stood outside with a watermelon.

"What a nice surprise," Russell said, taking the watermelon from my mother as she rushed into my apartment.

"They were on sale at *Shop Right*. I can't very well eat a whole huge watermelon," she said.

"Of course, you can't, Laverne." Russell pulled a knife from my silverware drawer and expertly sliced the watermelon. Next, he opened and passed my mother a beer.

"What's your favorite wing flavor?" I asked, handing my mom a plate.

Two weeks later, Lindsey, Claire, and Morgan walked into The Peaceful Rest.

"Hey Melody, just stopping in to say hi," Morgan said. He wrapped an arm around Claire, and she gazed up into his happy green eyes.

"I'm so glad you are feeling better. And, it's clear that something good came out of Stephanie seeking me out," I said, grinning at my new friend and my best friend.

"Yeah, we would have never met if it weren't for you," Morgan said.

"Oh, Morgan, can we tell her our good news?" Claire gushed.

I looked at Morgan.

"We're adopting," Claire blurted out.

"What?" I sputtered. The coffee J.J. had made came spitting out of my mouth, and it wasn't from the bitter taste. "You two have known each other for about three weeks."

"Not a human, Melody. A kitten. Lindsey just started volunteering at the Furry Friends Animal Shelter."

"It keeps my mind off Dave. We've separated but are working on things."

"Lindsey told us about this kitten named Bernie." Claire reached over and squeezed Lindsey's hand.

"Yeah, I knew they were the perfect couple for a kitten the moment I saw them," Lindsey said.

Claire opened up the pictures on her phone and proudly displayed a picture of Bernard, or little Bernie, as I affectionately called him.

"Claire is going to keep him at her place, but I can visit him whenever I want." Morgan looked down at the pictures with the joy of a new pet owner.

"It's so sad we lost Stephanie, but I'm glad we have all reconnected." I put my arms around both Lindsey and Claire.

"It's a shame we will never know why she came to see you," Claire said.

I looked around the drably decorated funeral home, its dimly lit lobby with its cream walls adorned with large portraits of Snugg's family and one of The Peaceful Rest when the roads were dirt. The funeral home in the picture with its brown sandstone exterior looked very similar to today, except that Arthur Snugg had put a porch on in the '80s and recently new carpet.

"I've been thinking. I bet she wanted to sell me her decorating services."

"You think she wanted to decorate the funeral home?" Claire started to laugh but then stopped and shook her head in agreement. "Melody Shore, I think you are right."

"I wonder what Stephanie would have done to the place?" I got up from my desk, picked my metal watering can off the shelf, filled it at the water fountain, and began watering the Peace Lilly. "I never thought after last week that things would go back to normal again here at Old Peaceful."

Arthur Snugg rushed into the funeral home, Alex and J.J. right behind him.

"Melody, a body is arriving, and I'm…"

"We're," Alex and J.J. said in unison, "pretty sure it's a murder victim."

"That's The Peaceful Rest," I said with as much lightness as I could muster. "It's never really peaceful."

The End.

Palacsinta (Hungarian Crepes)

4 large eggs
1 1/2 cups milk
1 pinch salt
1 teaspoon of sugar
1 cup all-purpose flour
1 tablespoon melted unsalted butter
(you will also need butter to coat the pan when cooking)

Some recipes for Palacsinta call for club soda or carbonated water. I don't use either, but I'm sure if you like either, you can find a recipe online that calls for this ingredient.

In a bowl, whisk the eggs with 1/2 cup of the milk and the salt. Whisk in the flour and sugar until smooth, then whisk in the remaining milk and the butter. Let the batter rest for 1 hour.

Turn your burner to medium and coat a 9"-10" non-stick pan with butter. Pour a small amount of batter into the pan and rotate it until it covers the bottom of the pan evenly. Cook until lightly browned on the bottom, about 30 seconds. Flip the crepe and cook the second side until brown dots appear, about 10 seconds longer. Transfer to a plate and repeat with the melted butter and remaining batter. Makes about 12 delicious crepes.

<u>Acknowledgments</u>

My family, friends, newsletter subscribers, and social media followers who enthusiastically inquired about a second Melody Shore book. You urged me to continue, and I am very grateful. My beta readers, Alice Heck, Paula Kurp, Donna Nardozi, and Sue Nath, I am so appreciative of your thoughts and catches. My writing friends at Sisters in Crime and all the children's authors that I am blessed to know and network with. You are so inspiring. To all of you readers ~ thank you all for allowing me to share with you a full-length Melody Shore mystery. I hope you enjoy reading this book as much as I enjoyed writing it.

Carole Lynn Jones's other mystery book is "**This New Job's Murder**," a collection of novella-length Melody Shore Mysteries. Her children's books are: "**The High-Flying, Water-Skiing, Magician Named Worm**" and "**The Hard-Working, Dirt-Moving, Garden-Helper Named Worm**." She is a member of Sisters in Crime and The Society of Children's Book Writers and Illustrators. "Writing is like solving a crime," she says. "You crack open the case, expose the motives, and then create a story that whistles in the dark." When she isn't writing, Carole spends her days and sometimes nights formatting legal documents for a large law firm in Pittsburgh, Pennsylvania. Married to her high school sweetheart, she enjoys spending time with her family and biking the many bike trails of Western Pennsylvania. Find her online at www.carolelynnjones.com.

Photo credit: Francine Smith, TimeSmart Images